Confessions of a Dyslexic Lover

RIA DUTTA

ISBN 978-93-9004-061-2
Copyright © Ria Dutta, 2022

First published in India 2022 by Leadstart Inkstate
A brand of One Point Six Technologies Pvt. Ltd.

123, Building J2, Shram Seva Premises,
Wadala Truck Terminal,
Mumbai 400022, Maharashtra, INDIA
Phone: +91 96999 33000
Email: info@leadstartcorp.com
www.leadstartcorp.com

Disclaimer: This is a work of fiction. All the names, characters, businesses, places, events and incidents in this book are either the product of the author's imagination or used in a fictitious manner. Any resemblance to actual persons, living or dead, or actual events is purely coincidental

Author's Disclaimer: The word 'dyslexic' is used as a creative and artistic expression and adds value to the story. It is not meant to offend anyone who is dyslexic. The author herself suffers from dyslexia as does the main character in the book.

Editor: Shayoni Mitra
Cover: Ashwini Rane
Layouts: Ashwini Rane

To the ones who lost themselves somewhere along the way...

You will find the road back to yourself one day.

ABOUT THE AUTHOR

Born in Calcutta (now Kolkata), Ria comes from a Bengali family. She currently resides in Bangalore and has been working as a content writer for the past six years. Growing up, she found her fondness for reading through the many books that lined the shelves at home. Her love for reading nurtured her passion for writing.

Confessions of a Dyslexic Lover is her first book through which she hopes to help people learn to understand, forgive, love and truly connect with themselves.

Acknowledgements

I would like to thank the entire team at Leadstart Publishing for helping me create this book and publish my story. I would like to thank my editor, Shayoni Mitra for having the patience to edit the many changes I kept making and in helping to make the book better and Naina Solanki from Leadstart who was the first one to like the manuscript and wanted to publish it. I would also like to thank Trupti Sawardekar (Head-Projects) and designers, Kshitij Dhawale and Ashwini Jadhav. Ananya Subramanian, my Project Manager, for her help and patience through the entire process of coordinating everything. And Bhavika Bharambe for her marketing efforts.

A big thank you to all the readers; I hope you enjoy reading the book as much as I enjoyed writing it. Thank you to all my friends and my family, especially my 10-year-old niece who helped me edit a paragraph and provided her innocent and adorable inputs in making the story better.

A heartfelt thank you to my best friend for conceptualizing and creating the perfect cover for the book.

And last but not the least; I would like to thank my sources of inspiration …

Author's Note

Just like the main character's faults, her story is not perfect. So, readers, keep a lookout for mistakes in the text (errors in punctuations, grammar and more) to add to a unique reading experience that mirrors her chaotic imperfect life.

TRIGGER WARNING: This book touches upon several dark topics such as abuse and suicide. Reader discretion is advised.

Chapter 1

ADAM

With a red rose peeping out of his jacket pocket and a bag full of gifts hanging from the bike's handle, Adam was on his way to meet the girl of his dreams. She was everything he had ever wanted; she was funny, sweet, caring and the most beautiful girl he had ever laid eyes on. Her big brown eyes, her wavy hair, her soft pink lips and the way it curved into the most mesmerizing smile – he was hooked.

He knew she was the one. He had always known this right from their college days. They had attended undergrads together in the same college where he met her for the first time after which, they ended up going to the same university for their post-graduation. He spoke to her a couple of times and discovered that she came from a Bengali family. She and her parents moved to Chicago from Kolkata, India, when she was in high school and since then, for the last fourteen years she'd been living in the States. Her Bengali name was Aayena, meaning mirror, but after moving to the U.S all her friends called her Anna, as it was easier for them to pronounce. So it became a nickname she grew fond of and stuck with.

This was the same case with him; his original Punjabi name was Aadat, meaning habit, which was changed to Adam by his friends here in the States, so he went with it.

Anna was always the pretty, popular girl right from high school, who everyone wanted to be with, but the best thing about her was despite being so beautiful she never let it get to her head. She was always kind and nice to everyone. She was an angel; she was unlike anything Adam had ever seen before. Though she had been with someone else at the time, Adam was still hung up on her and he knew it was wishful thinking that she'd ever look his way.

Eventually they started hanging out a lot more because she had broken up with the guy she was seeing and was now dating one of Adam's close friends. An instant friendship struck and they became the best of friends from then onwards. It was during this time he got to learn so much about her. Her likes, dislikes, her short temper and her dyslexia. She had been severely dyslexic since childhood. But over the years it had gotten a lot better, but math and logical reasoning was something she could never understand.

In due time her relationship with his buddy soured and eventually, they broke up with good reason. He never did treat her right... he was physically and verbally abusive towards her; she was definitely better off without him. Despite Adam and her other friends advising her to end the relationship, she still kept running back to him. It hurt Adam to see her like that, but he was helpless because she would listen to no one. After the relationship ended, Adam thought about telling her how he felt, but like always he held back and took the backseat of being the best friend.

She always did have a way with men, everyone seemed to want her. She made her mistakes, and there were lots… and Adam was always there with her through it all – never judgemental; always the shoulder to cry on. But a friend was all he was, up until their post-graduation days, and he couldn't believe his luck; out of all the men, she had finally chosen to be with him! He was never the ladies' man, he had had his crushes but he had never approached anyone, but now his luck had changed for the better and he wasn't going to let anything get in the way of that.

He finally had her… all of her; for the last six years, or at least that's what he hoped. She was quite unpredictable, always changing her mind and getting a little crazy now and then, but she was so playful, he could be himself around her, his real self, in all his crazy glory. When they were together, they wouldn't have a care in the world and return right back to the carefree childhood days of laughter and playing pretend. Despite these childish escapes they still managed to keep the passion alive in their relationship, it was the perfect mix of both worlds – childish play and adult fun; and he couldn't get enough.

Despite this perfect world, there was always the one thing he feared; one day she would walk away from him; she would realize that she could do better, stop loving him, and move away… He wasn't wrong to think this. He had faced a lot of heartbreak during their time together; she was going through a rough phase and ended up doing things she had regretted, it broke him into pieces every time, but he always forgave her. However, she was a changed woman now, and for the past two years their relationship had been a stable one. But he couldn't help but wonder if she would repeat her pattern again, and if she did, would he forgive her another time or let her go for good – trust once broken is hard to fix, and she had broken it four times. Could he forgive her again? What kind of man would that make him, a coward? A loser? A man with no self- respect?

He had faith in her, but his faith wavered now and then when she talked to another man: the married man at work who kept hitting on her, some of her ex-boyfriends and basically just any man he saw had his eyes on her. Most of the time he would not let these things bother him. But at times when he was all alone at night his mind would drift to those days when he was left broken by her actions and lies. Had she completely come out of that? Was she capable of cheating again? These thoughts haunted him and he wished he could just get them out of his head completely. He had come a long way, the nightmares, anxiety and cold sweats in the middle of the night had stopped, that's the kind of impact she had had on him. There was still a long way to go when it came to giving away all of his trust to her again. Sometimes he wondered if she was dyslexic even when it came to knowing herself and what and who she truly wanted.

These past two months, when they had been away from each other, those nightmares came back to him every night. It was the same feeling of loss and desperation, and he wondered why they had started up again because things were going well with them.

He decided to push all these negative thoughts away for now; he was going to meet her soon. She had just come back home after a long vacation with her friends and he too had come back a day earlier from his vacation with his family. He couldn't wait to meet her and surprise her. She wasn't the biggest fan of surprises and he was a bit worried, considering the time was 11 pm, usually when she started prepping for bed. But he thought, this time could be an exception, since they hadn't seen each other in two months.

He finally reached her place, parked his bike and dialled her number with his heart racing.

Chapter 2

ANNA

She had just taken out her belly ring and was about to change into her PJ's when her phone rang, it was Adam. They had spoken on the phone earlier and said their goodnights so she wondered why he was calling again, she hoped everything was alright. She picked up the phone with a touch of worry in her voice "Hey what's up? What happened?"

Adam replied in a playful tone, "Look out of your window." Anna rushed to the window to see Adam and his motorbike parked right outside her house. Her first reaction was one of pure joy, the usual feeling she had every time she saw his face, but then reality hit her and she had this horrible feeling in the pit of her stomach and her mind raced through the events that had taken place over the past two months.

She had been dreading meeting Adam, she needed more time to prepare herself. Too much had happened and if she went down now, he would see right through her. When it came to her, Adam always had a sixth sense… and she knew, if she went down, everything would be over. What was she to do? She was in a fix…if she didn't go down something would seem off and if she did go down, then too things would go wrong. She took a deep breath and slowly let the events of the past two months sink in.

It all started from the time Adam went back home for a month-long break. He had just about had it with his job and needed some time out to de-stress. She wasn't too happy about him leaving her alone and taking off, because most of her life, since her early teens, she had always needed someone by her side. A relationship to lean on for comfort and support. She never had an understanding of who she really was, having always jumped from one relationship to another because of her fear of being alone. She had practically made up her mind that she wouldn't be alright without someone always assuring her that they love her; she craved love, and she never understood why.

She had dyslexia as a child and it still pestered her now at the age of twenty-eight, especially with calculations. Sometimes she even wondered if she was dyslexic when it came to love and relationships as well.

She knew she was being cowardly, but she was just too afraid to even try to be on her own, be single. She didn't even know what that was like because ever since the age of fourteen she was always in a relationship.

So, when it was time for Adam to go, she was not too thrilled, but she knew it was what he needed and so she let him go. The first week went by smoothly but by the time the second week rolled around she was already feeling distant from him.

It all started with a harmless conversation with a man at the office. Anna and Adam both worked in a small start-up company called Wordplay. The place was run by a husband-wife duo. Adam handled sales and marketing while Anna took the lead in scripting content for their clients. The company was only three years old and both Anna and Adam had been working there for a year. Now, this man at the office wasn't just a co-worker, he was the husband who co-owned the company. He was friendly and charming. Adam and another colleague were not very fond of him and always kept warning Anna that he was a little too friendly with her. Anna at the beginning didn't feel this way, but now and then she would see the way he looked at her, lustfully… and his compliments were always flattering.

His wife was a very sweet lady with whom Anna used to interact a lot, so she didn't think much of his ways and just blew it off as harmless flirting. He always used to motivate Anna to make something great of herself and focus on her career and she appreciated this quality of his.

He was one of the few people Anna had let in on a passion project she was working on, and he had promised to help her with it, since he had a great network of contacts. Since Anna was their lead writer, he too wanted her help with content on a campaign for Wordplay which would require her to work extra hours, as this was a separate project from her usual daily work with their clients. They decided to meet and discuss the plan of action.

The first meeting was innocent, with some coffee and conversations; it was from the second meeting that things began to go downhill. The early evenings turned to late ones and the coffee switched to wine… it was during one of these meetings, Anna got a good look at him. He was pretty cute.

But she was not about to have an affair with a married man, she had her morals intact when it came to this. She had made a lot of mistakes in the past but this by far would have been the worst.

As Anna was reflecting on her ethical stance, he stopped what he was saying and looked intently into her eyes as if reading her mind and said, "I have a confession to make… I've been attracted to you from the first time I laid my eyes on you. You are so sexy and so beautiful, and it's been so hard for me to hold myself back, but it feels good to finally be able to tell you this." Anna responded with a shy smile and said, "That's sweet, but you are married and this wouldn't be right. You shouldn't act on it; maybe in another life we could have given this a shot, because I think you're a really wonderful man. But for now, let it go, because you don't want to look back at your life and have any regrets, right?"

He smiled and said, "You're right Anna, but what if we did it just one time, the first and last time? Would you sleep with me right now if you could?"

He was so direct, she thought, and kind of creepy. "No, I wouldn't," she said. "Ok Anna, you're a good girl and you're very mature I must say," he said. This was something Anna was not used to hearing. She was always known as the crazy, impulsive, girl. "Thanks," she replied.

After dinner, he volunteered to show her the new office space he had bought, which was a couple of blocks away. He told her they were expanding the company and had just finished work on this office space and would love for Anna to see it. Anna had a slight inkling that something wasn't right, but she brushed it aside and decided not to overthink things. After all, she had made her stance clear; surely he understood.

After a few minutes, they reached the place. It was decorated with wall hangings, paintings and indoor plants. It was surely a step up from the office she worked at and made for a cute and quirky workspace.

Before Anna had a chance to express her appreciation, she saw him lock the door shut with the keys from the corner of her eye. Anna began to say something, but before she could start, he swept her into his arms and kissed her. The kisses came strong and hard at first, his hands were all over her body, grabbing her. It was as if he was finally breaking free and reaching out for the one thing he had longed for… for so long, and he couldn't control himself.

After a while, they moved from the entrance to the board room and the kisses became more gentle and loving. He slowly pulled down her dress and looked at her body and said, "God you are beautiful …" and before Anna could respond, he had lifted her on top of the board room table. She felt him under her dress, and told him to stop. She had told him they shouldn't do this, back at the restaurant, and she repeated it even now, but he didn't seem to listen. The more she resisted and said "no", the more he forced himself on her saying it'd just be this one time.

She didn't feel right with him touching her. This was forced and not what she wanted… then why was her body betraying her thoughts and emotions? Why wasn't she able to muster up any strength to fight him off, to push him away? She was frozen in fear – paralysed.

He now pulled her off the table and on to the floor on her knees, she knew she couldn't run because the door was locked. This realization made her feel even more helpless. There was nowhere to run, she was a strong girl, there was so much she could do at that moment – kick, punch, bite, scream… but she was unable to move, her weak protests had also stopped now; she had given up. She felt sick, there was a sensation deep within her, like a nasty prick, something burned, she hoped this would end soon and it did, it was over within seconds.

He got off her, she stumbled trying to stand up, "I told you I didn't want this, you didn't listen! And it's so disgusting… the way this happened… what does this make me now? How must you see me now?" The irony at this moment was truly disappointing. After being violated, Anna was the one feeling dirty and wondering what he thought of her, while he felt nothing and never even questioned his character. "Don't worry baby, I don't think anything bad of you. In fact, I think we should head to Bali for a vacation just you and me and the sun and the sea," he smiled.

Was he serious? Anna wondered. She told him she needed to get home. At that moment his wife called, but he didn't answer. She kept calling him... Anna told him she really needed to leave and had already booked a cab which was almost here. He finally got the key from his back pocket and unlocked the door while picking up his wife's call, he winked and smiled at Anna while she was leaving. Anna did not smile back; she got out of the office with quick strides, onto the road and into her cab; without looking back. The situation still hadn't sunk in. Maybe she wanted it… that's why it happened, maybe she liked it and that's why she let it happen. That's why she didn't fight hard enough… it was her fault, she was a slut, a whore. She had been called these names time and again in the past by her ex-boyfriends and the girls who had hated her in school. She had a terrible reputation, and why wouldn't she? She had cheated so many times. What would happen if the guy she was with left her or died? Who would love her then? She needed someone else to take his place so she could be loved, a backup in case something went wrong. It was crazy how twisted she was… she really had no idea why she craved to be loved this much and why she was so afraid to be on her own.

She stood under the shower for an hour but still didn't feel clean. She barely slept that night and when she reached office the next day, he looked at her like he wanted to tear off all her clothes.

She still took his calls and found the gifts he'd sneak into her bag when she wasn't at her desk. She always made up some excuse to not meet him though he kept asking her to meet up or plan a getaway somewhere. Anna wondered if his wife not being able to have kids was the reason for him to have an extramarital affair, so she asked him one day and his reply left her flabbergasted, "I'm very happy in my marriage, I just find you too attractive and I can't help myself." What a selfish human being! Anna thought to herself.

Anna was a crier and would cry over just about anything, but this time, she was so shocked that she was unable to cry after this incident. It took her a week to finally realize what had happened. It was not until she confided in two of her best girlfriends, Sophie and Chrissy, that she realized the extent of the violation. After letting the matter sink in, she finally broke down in tears. She blocked him on every platform, threw away the gifts and threatened him to stay away from her, or she would tell everyone, including his wife, what he had done. She couldn't work there anymore, nor could she bear to see him every day. She couldn't file a lawsuit against him because she had no proof and it would be a long-drawn humiliating process, one where the woman's character and her choices are dragged through the mud. It was for this reason so many victims refused to speak up. This was the sad reality but Anna just didn't have the strength to go through the mortifying ordeal. She also loved her job; despite being dyslexic, she had always been a good writer and was often praised for her work; therefore, the decision to resign left her feeling even more broken.

This is the time Anna decided she needed a getaway with her friends. She knew she could count on them. They had always been great friends to her and she needed them now more than ever. So, it was set, Sophie, Chrissy, Dan and Anna, would be heading to Dubai the following week. Hopefully, they would all get leave from work. In fact, that was the only thing that could ruin their plans; Anna kept her fingers crossed.

She had known Dan, Sophie and Chrissy since her post-graduation days. There was an instant friendship that formed between the girls on the very first day of university; Adam hadn't been around for the first week since he was down with the flu, so Anna had been by herself. The girls were seated next to each other during orientation and their mutual dislike towards the boring speech being given by the Dean helped them strike up a conversation. They later realized they had all signed up for almost the same classes and hence the trio became inseparable.

Sophie was the cute and peppy brunette, the 'mom' of their group always making sure everyone was being responsible and safe, she especially worried for Anna and her reckless ways and Anna appreciated how protective she was of her. Chrissy was the wild red head, always the life of the party; fun and carefree, her positive, fun-loving personality was something Anna admired.

And then there was Anna, the destructive, dramatic, crazy one. She wondered sometimes why her friends tolerated her.

Dan joined their group much later, around the time they were in their second semester. He was in Chrissy's drama class and was very shy, he didn't speak much and didn't have too many friends because of his introvert nature. He was more of a loner, but by being around Chrissy so much, he slowly started opening up to people and soon became friends with Anna and Sophie too.

It wasn't until Anna had broken up with her abusive ex that he confessed his feelings towards her, she was desperate to get over her ex so she tried to force herself to have feelings for Dan. She went out with him couple of times, they even shared a kiss. She tried to love his light auburn curls and his grey eyes but her heart was just not in it. She started seeing other guys and then eventually dated Adam and told Dan that they were better off as friends.

But Dan was still in love with her and very protective of her, so she decided against telling him about what had happened at work.

And coming clean with Adam was not an option because he would not forgive her this time; and he would kill that guy, instead, Anna decided to not tell him anything, not even the fact that she had just quit her job.

It turned out that luck was on Anna's side this time around and everyone got leave for a solid three weeks, they were all headed for some fun in the Middle East. Anna couldn't wait, she knew this is exactly what she needed, to clear her head and heal her body, mind and soul to move on from this dark time.

But one thing she promised herself this time was to stay away from men! No matter how cute they were, and how much attention they gave her, she was going to steer clear of them and nothing or no one was going to stop this from happening.

Chapter 3

ANNA

After thirteen hours of bad Airplane food, a sore butt and practically zero sleep, Anna and her friends were welcomed by the bright sunshine of the dessert and the gleaming tops of the skyscrapers. Anna forgot all about her restless sleep and was immediately invigorated by the bustling energy all around her; she couldn't get off the aircraft fast enough!

The beauty of Dubai was spectacular – the golden desert speckled with skyscrapers, blue oceans with pearly white sands and all things luxurious, were the reasons Anna and her friends chose this tourist hotspot as their holiday destination.

Everything about the place appealed to her. The second she stepped out of the airport she felt like she was breathing in a different air; fresher air that was filling up her body and mind with positivity and happiness. She couldn't imagine being anywhere else but here.

The first week was just as she had hoped, if not better. From dancing all night at the hottest clubs to ice skating at the mall, Anna and her friends left no stones unturned when it came to having fun. There was a lot of retail therapy and delicious delicacies involved on this trip as well. Anna knew she was making a rather large dent in her wallet but she didn't really care. After a very long time, she was finally starting to feel like herself again. This was a new feeling, and she was enjoying it.

She did miss Adam a lot, he would call each day at least once, and they would talk. There were a lot of hot guys all around. They were some of the most gorgeous guys she had ever laid eyes on checking her out, some even came by for a chat, but she stood her ground and stayed strong. She had told herself no men and she was sticking to that decision.

After a week of pure bliss and an expanding waistline Anna had never felt better. She didn't care about her diet, or fitting into a specific dress size, or even if any man noticed her. She just did whatever she wanted to and whatever made her happy, without someone telling her otherwise. This was a refreshing change for Anna and she was loving every moment of it.

The second week rolled in with the same excitement, Anna and her friends decided to head out to the desert for some dune surfing. With every twist and turn of the jeep they went surfing through the sandy dunes of the desert under the saffron evening sun. Anna's tummy filled with butterflies; the good kind; she and her friends were being hurled in opposite directions of the jeep as it went on top of a big dune and came rushing back down. This was one exhilarating experience Anna was sure she was never going to forget.

After the dune surfing was over all the different jeeps headed for the heart of the desert where more excitement awaited their arrival, in the form of camel rides, belly dancers and mouth-watering dishes. Anna was the first to get on the camel; the last time she had probably been on one was when she was a kid. When she and her parents lived in India, they had visited the historic city of Agra to see the spectacular Taj Mahal, she still remembered wearing her purple tights and matching Barbie tee that day and being a little afraid to get on the camel. The photograph captured her crooked body, almost falling off the camel, nervously smiling at the camera; that was a great day; it was a great trip. All her trips with her parents were amazing and she always had such fun on them. They were good old times of happiness and innocence. She couldn't remember the last time she had gone anywhere with her parents. The last fourteen years she had been so busy with school, college, work, friends and boys, she never did take much time out for them. A sense of sadness swept over her; they were growing old. She decided after flying back home she'd plan another trip, this time with her parents.

Back on the camel, Anna looked around at the vast stretch of land laden with golden sand and the spectacular setting sun on the horizon. She took out her phone to capture the view when her eyes fell on something, rather someone, familiar in the distance. She squinted and leaned in for a closer look and that's when she spotted him. At first, she thought was she dreaming… or was it one of those mirages? But when he turned around and locked eyes with her, she knew he was real.

In complete panic, Anna dropped her phone, and in an attempt to save her phone, she too fell off the camel and onto the sand! Luckily the sand was soft, so she didn't get hurt. They had just begun their journey and weren't too far from where the camp was set up, so she decided to make a run for it, back to camp before he made his way towards her. Running on the sand was not easy and she knew she looked like a big floppy bird but she didn't care. She had to get away from there!

She reached the camp's bathroom sweaty and breathless, all she could think was, *what was he doing here? Why him, why now, why God WHY?!* She had to focus; she had to calm down and go out there. Her friends were already gathered outside the door, they had seen what had happened and wanted to find out if she was ok. *"Breathe Anna breathe, maybe he didn't see you, get a grip you can't stay in here forever you have got to get out there,"* she told herself. She took one last deep breath and opened the door.

"He's here," Anna told her friends as soon as she opened the door. "Who's here?" Sophie asked. "Mike," said Anna. They all looked at each other in alarm. "You mean Mike, who you haven't spoken to in two years after you told him you wished he was dead?" asked Sophie.

"Yes, that Mike. Only we have been chatting now and then for the past couple of months since he reached out to me, but I had no idea he was here though," Anna explained. "You've been talking to him again, after how he treated you? Anna, come on!" Dan said exasperated.

"People change you know, and he seems to have matured over the last two years, but anyway that's beside the point, I'm not ready to meet him right now, plus he just saw me fall off a camel, how embarrassing is that! What in God's name is he doing here anyway?!" Anna screamed.

"Well he is a pilot and does travel around the world so maybe his flight landed in Dubai and he's here just enjoying the place," Chrissy added. Anna knew she was right and she also knew she wasn't ready to face him, but she had no choice, he had seen her before she foolishly fell off the camel, plus they still had the belly dancing show and dinner to complete as a part of the package before they were escorted back to the hotel, so there was no escaping this, she just had to face him. As she started to prepare herself mentally, Sophie looking alarmed said, "Umm Anna I think we have company…" Anna looked up to see Mike headed straight in their direction, just one look at his big broad chest and confident stride and Anna knew she was in trouble… *again.*

Chapter 4

MIKE

God, she looked as beautiful as he had last seen her, maybe even more, if that was even possible. The shorts she was wearing showed off her long lean legs and that T-shirt hugged all the right curves. If she only realised how truly beautiful she was. Why couldn't she see what everyone else always saw when they looked at her? He never understood women and Anna, in particular, was a complete mystery to him. A mystery he tried solving many a time but failed miserably. Maybe it was his fault, maybe it was hers; maybe the both of them were to blame. Everything was all wrong with them and yet everything felt so right.

He wasn't used to feeling this way, so lost and uncertain. He was a man of confidence and power, he functioned on focus and hard work, and it's these qualities that got him to where he was today. He had always wanted to fly and was now a well-respected pilot, he loved his job and the perks that came with it. He was happy and rich, content with his life, but there was always this sense of emptiness, this void and he knew the reason for it – Anna. It had always been her.

Apart from being strikingly beautiful and fun to be around, one thing was for sure, as long as you were around Anna, you'd never be bored, she was very entertaining. She had this childish air about her, she was like a little girl just wanting to play and have fun, but at the same time she could flip a switch and become this sensual sexy woman that he just had to have; she was something else.

But the one thing that kept Mike hooked onto Anna for the past eleven years was her ability to make him feel invincible, he didn't know whether she did this intentionally or it came naturally to her, but she had always made him feel like he was a man, a real man, a hero, a protector; someone so strong that nothing could ever destroy him. No other woman had ever made him feel this way. He had had many affairs in different parts of the world, and yes, they were fun and had their charm. Each woman he had been with had her beauty and wit and he had always had a good time.

But after being around the world and having been with so many gorgeous women, he still never got over Anna. His jealousy was always at its peak when he was with her, he wanted to knock out any guy who looked at her, talked to her, hit on her and there were always guys like that around Anna right from when he'd known her in high school. He had to have her for himself, that's what he had always hoped and wished for until things took a turn for the worst.

He had noticed that there was a guy among Anna's friends he wondered if he was her boyfriend, this thought itself made him boil with rage. That was the other thing about Anna... a girl like her was never single. Men were drawn to her like a moth to a flame. But she too needed that emotional support, that love and attention which he was not able to give her because his job always took him away from her and she wasn't the type of girl to wait around, she always needed someone to be with her.

Well, he was with her now, fate had brought them both to the exact same location. The warm desert air had cooled down now and a blanket of stars had lit up the night sky, there couldn't have been a more romantic setting. He was sure he had made her nervous. That fall off the camel was so Anna and also such a clear sign that he still had a shot… unless that guy turned out to be her boyfriend. But that hadn't stopped her before… but then again, it had been two years; things change, people change.

He still had a sliver of hope. If she was surprised enough to fall off that camel, surely there was still something deep inside her heart for him, because he was sure he still had feelings for her, despite her nastiness the last time they had spoken. He was so mad at her that night… how could she have said all those things to him? At one point he even thought, he hated her, but he's the one who had reached out to her recently, because despite everything he still missed her and still loved her.

He got closer and noticed her face, just like before, he could see the red hues creeping up on her cheeks, and she couldn't meet his eyes, this gave him the clear signal that she was still into him, so he still had a chance maybe, just maybe… But he wasn't sure; he needed to get closer to her to find out what she was thinking. But that was the thing about her, he could never understand what was on her mind, she would say one thing one day and then change her mind and do something completely opposite the next, she was indecisive and unpredictable.

Was that something he wanted to get into again? All the drama and chaos? Well, he was going to find out soon enough.

Chapter 5

ANNA

"Hey, well this is a surprise!" said Mike reaching out to hug Anna. Anna was just about to reach for a shake and they both ended up in an awkward collision. "Come on we can do better than that!" Mike said and gave Anna a big bear hug, and for a while, they just stayed in that embrace; Anna wasn't ready to let go yet. She felt safe in his arms, he was so big and strong and warm and tall, and his smell was intoxicating. He had this particular Mike smell, his natural scent mixed with his cologne, made the best smell in the world – a scent that was familiar yet forgotten, it took her back to another time and nostalgia struck. She wasn't willing to let that feeling go, but a loud "Ahem!" from Dan's direction made them both let go of each other.

Anna and her friends got acquainted with Mike's buddies, and Anna's friends with Mike as well. Anna couldn't help but notice the tiny frames on most of the girls on his crew. They were slim, had a great sense of fashion and knew how to apply make-up the right way. Anna couldn't help but feel a bit insecure, she knew she had put on some weight, she never had a good sense of fashion, anything black was her go-to always and her make-up skills were almost non-existent, she couldn't even put on lipstick without getting some on her teeth or apply kohl on her eyes with a steady hand! So, it was natural for her to feel a little out of place. Luckily, she had her friends right there with her. She wondered how many of these girls Mike had been with, but she tried to dismiss the thought.

There were just two other guys on the crew and they weren't bad to look at either, they too were well-built, groomed and seemed to have a good fashion sense, but Anna's eyes were set only on Mike.

They were all gathered around the fire eating their delicious dinner, Mike and Anna were in deep conversation, when out came the belly dancers, Anna just couldn't catch a break tonight! But Mike did not be seem to be affected by any other women there; he was completely taken by Anna.

They spoke a lot about his journeys, her life in general, her job; though she did leave out the bit about the latest incident that had taken place because she knew he would judge her and blame her for getting herself into that situation and tell her it was her fault. "So, is there a boyfriend in the picture at the moment?" he inquired. Anna thought of Adam, should she say his name or just say that she's single? "Nope," she replied. "I find that really hard to believe, a girl like you being single is pretty rare." Anna was not sure if he was complimenting her or taking a dig at her. "Why is it so hard to believe?" she asked annoyed. "Well because you're fucking gorgeous! You're the entire package... guys wouldn't be stupid enough to leave you alone, trust me, I know," he winked. That made Anna blush again and she couldn't meet his eye. It had taken her three drinks to finally make eye contact with him. This was a problem from the very start, his look was always so intense she wasn't able to look into his eyes without feeling a sense of extreme thrill, but also a sense of nervousness, she would be so overwhelmed with emotion that'd she'd start blushing and look away. She always felt like those stereotypically shy Bollywood actresses in old movies when she was around him.

And this time too her behaviour must have given Mike the signal that he still had an impact on her, a big impact. She loved the attention he was giving her, and he had eyes only for her though they were surrounded by such beautiful women; that made her feel happy. They had strayed away from the group and walked off into the desert, not too far, but far enough to get some privacy. He held her hand under the moonlit desert sky speckled with stars, the moment was right out of a romantic movie; it was perfect.

He stopped walking and held her from behind, buried his face in her hair and her neck and took a nice long whiff; he loved smelling her as much as she loved smelling him. Anna felt his warm breath on her ears and neck which sent an electric shock all over her body. Her goosebumps were visible and she didn't even make an effort to hide them from him. He spun her around and before she knew it, he had brought down his lips on hers and they started kissing passionately.

Every cell in her body was on fire; bursting with excitement. His hands were moving all over her body, feeling every inch of her. She wanted him right there in the middle of the desert, she couldn't contain herself. But she knew they didn't have enough time, so she stopped kissing him and backed away, he pulled her right back into him and they started to kiss again. Her head was spinning and her heart was throbbing.

"We have to stop, it's almost time to leave," she said breathlessly. Just then the tour guide blew his whistle to let the crowd know that they had to leave, it was as if he had almost heard Anna. She was grateful in a way to get away from Mike because she was starting to lose control again and she needed to get a hold of herself. She began backing away but he picked her up and wouldn't let go, "Just a few more minutes please, I can't get enough of you," he exclaimed. She was defenceless against his strength and she caved in. They stayed in lip-lock for some more time until Anna heard her friends calling out for her. Finally, they let go of each other. Before making their way back, Anna noticed Mike kiss her shoulder and smack his lips, like he had just tasted something really good. She had noticed this about him every time they had been together. On the walk back to camp she asked him why he did this and he said, "I lick the taste of you off my lips so that my tongue can savour it long after you leave.". These things Mike said sometimes, always made Anna feel so sexy and good about herself – a feeling she wasn't used to.

Anna had told Mike that he cannot spend the night at her hotel. Also, there was no way she was going to go back to his hotel room and jump into bed with him on the first night. She needed to get her head straightened out, this holiday was about her, and she had done such a good job staying away from men so far, but Mike had to come along and ruin everything. How did she let this happen?

Mike and she had decided to meet the next evening for dinner; she would just tell him then that nothing could happen between them by informing him about Adam, hopefully, he would understand and leave her alone, but did she really want him to?

Chapter 6

MIKE

Mike barely slept a wink that night, all he wanted to do was run his hands all over Anna's body, her skin was so soft and her smell was so intoxicating, her natural scent mixed with the perfume she was wearing just about made the best smell in the world. He was hooked on her and wanted so much more but she refused to come back to the room with him. He knew she wanted him… but he wondered why she didn't just come back with him. She said she was single and that Dan guy was just her friend but he was sure that Dan had feelings for her considering the death glares he was giving Mike the entire night.

Maybe she had a boyfriend back home she didn't want him to know about. Mike knew her and he knew she had always needed a man, someone to love and hold her; that was one of her biggest weaknesses. Frankly, he couldn't put himself in her shoes and understand this flawed character trait, because he was the complete opposite; strong, independent and never needed to rely on anyone else for emotional stability. The only person he had let in emotionally was Anna, all his ego and pride always took a back seat when it came to her.

Anna was one of the few people who knew his real name; Mikesh, meaning King of Lord. She knew, like her, his parents were Bengali as well and had moved to the U.S when he was just a baby. However, when he was only two years old, his mom walked out on them for another man and eventually his dad re-married an American lady. He adored his step-mum. She loved children and wanted to have a son and name him Mike. But since she discovered she could never have any kids of her own, Mike decided to change his name for her.

From the time they had known each other, Mike was an open-book to Anna, he let her in on all his secrets and his emotions.

But where did all of that get him? Her saying, he should have died instead of Jake… and that destroyed him, that hit a little too close to home. Back in high school he had come between Jake and Anna. Jake had been his best friend. They had known each other since kindergarten when Jake had walked up to Mike demanding to know why his skin colour was darker than his and everyone else's in class. Mike had been the only brown kid in that class, but that didn't really bother him till Jake brought it up. When he couldn't come up with a fitting reply Jake had said to him, "I think it's because when cocoa mixes with milk it makes the best drink in the world – hot chocolate! Just like that, God made us for each other. You are cocoa and I am milk. So when we get together, we will be the bestest friends in the world!" He then gave a toothy grin and held Mike's hand; they both smiled at each and never left each other's side since. Until high school that is, when Jake and Anna had first started going out. Mike was happy for him, he even bought Jake his first pack of condoms, since Jake was apprehensive about buying them himself. And he was always the mediator in the fights between Jake and Anna. He made sure he helped them patch things up because he liked the two of them together; she was good for him. Mike thought Anna was beautiful of course but didn't have any feelings for her. It was only after this one trip with his buddies over the weekend when he came back to school on a Monday morning, the first thing he saw when he entered school was Anna standing in their school balcony on the fourth floor. She looked so beautiful… almost angelic, just standing there in the sunshine.

She looked down at him and gave a little wave and smiled and he knew, that was the exact moment he fell for her! Something about that moment felt like magic. He knew coming between them was not right but he just wanted her so much. So, he made his move and she responded, but not completely. She still held on to Jake, but she couldn't let go of Mike either. She was always so confused, never truly knowing what she wanted. It was a mess and they hurt Jake.

Jake dying in a car accident four years back had crushed Anna and had left Mike quite broken too. Jake wasn't even driving, his cousin was at the wheel, driving back from a friend's house, and neither of them were under the influence. The roads were slippery because of the rain. Jake wanted to play a song on his phone but his cousin wanted to listen to something else, so instead of keeping an eye on the road, they both were childishly caught up in a silly argument, each trying to grab the phone. In this tug-or-war they both missed the dog in the middle of the street and by the time they realized and his cousin slammed the brakes and turned the car away from the dog, it was too late! The car couldn't take the sudden impact and swerved on the slippery road. They missed the dog but went crashing into a truck that was coming from the other side. The truck driver wasn't able to pull the brakes on time; the vehicles collided with each other. But it was the passengers of the car that were affected the most. Because of the impact both Jake and his cousin hit their heads on the windshield, but only Jake's head broke through the windshield and then took another blow by hitting the bumper of the truck, crushing his skull leading to a brain haemorrhage. By the time the paramedics arrived, it was too late, Jake had suffered severe brain injury which had caused internal bleeding ultimately leading to his death. His cousin, suffered a head injury too, but not as severe, and managed to survive after a long surgery. Anna had been completely devastated for months and she kept having recurring dreams about Jake's happy face dripping with blood. She couldn't eat, or sleep and was a mess for months; Mike went through the same thing minus the dreams.

He wished he and Anna could have been there for each other during this time. But when this incident happened, he was in his flight training in Chicago and she was away at college in New York. Eventually they got better, but this would always be something that left a sense of emptiness in their hearts.

Now, it had been four years since the accident and eleven years since that day he saw her on the balcony and he still felt the same way about her.

But there was that time in-between when they had been together and she had been loyal for once in her life. And he had been the one who had been bad to her. But she would drive him mad, push his buttons, make him angry during fights. She would not let him walk away from the situation and instead would want to sort it out though he wanted to leave – how selfish she was; maybe still is. She could never give him what he wanted and that loud voice of hers drove him up the roof, especially during fights.

What he had done to her was wrong, but she pushed his

buttons and he couldn't help himself. He wanted a partner who would take care of him but all he could see in her was a stupid, immature, selfish, petulant child who he had to take care of. She frustrated him and he couldn't respect her because what had she done to earn his respect? She was dumb and completely lacked common sense; she was disobedient and didn't listen to him and argued back; she was messy; she was too emotional and sensitive and loud. She was not independent; she was immature; she was practically useless, but still, he loved her right? And yes, he had been wrong to curse, criticize and hit her but, she had it coming. She needed to be put in her place.

Plus, she had hurt him over the years, she was not single, always with another, while still allowing him to flirt with her and flirting back over the phone while he was away. She even believed some friend of hers who told her lies about him and she used that as an excuse to stop talking to him. After convincing her to come back, she agreed and started dating him, but then left again. Hence, what Mike had done in comparison was not as bad as what she'd done to him, they were just moments of angry outbursts and nothing else. In a way she deserved it.

But after putting up with all her nonsense, she left him and he was the one who had reached out to her after two years… what was it about this girl that always made him come crawling back to her?

Chapter 7

ANNA

Talking to Adam was torture that night; she barely dared to say love you back. She hardly slept that night. The next morning was spent trying to pick out something nice to wear for dinner and the afternoon catching up on a little sleep. Why did she feel the need to look good while telling Mike that nothing can happen between them? Was it to taunt him a little; torture him – maybe it was her guilty pleasure.

Or maybe she knew that if he made any advances, she might not have the will to fight him off, so she was just preparing herself to look her best when things went down. Not even she could figure herself out. What a mess she truly was! Her phone buzzed and she saw a message from Mike, "I want to run my fingers along all the curves and crevices of your body... to feel every inch of you," Anna wanted that too; she didn't know how she would be able to control herself when she met him, but she had to try.

Her friends were not happy about her going to see Mike, especially Dan. Despite having told Dan they should be friends he refused to understand, and it was annoying at times, but he was a great friend who always came to her rescue whenever she needed it, and she didn't want to lose his friendship because she really did value him a lot; otherwise she wouldn't have asked him to tag along on this trip.

The three girls were in Anna's room as she got ready for her meeting with Mike. Sophie was worried for Anna, "Look Anna you have been through a lot lately, and Mike isn't exactly Prince Charming, he's definitely not the worst, but he has done some pretty questionable things in the past. I don't think you need this right now, remember this entire trip was about focusing on yourself. Plus hello! What about Adam? Think of him Anna. I think you should call him and cancel... say whatever you have to on the phone and let him go," she requested.

Chrissy on the other hand advised, "Oh come on Sophie, yes agreed Mike's not right for her, but Anna there's no harm in having a little fun you know, you don't have to get into a relationship with him. After all you've been through; you deserve to have a little fun with someone you're so attracted too. Sex can be therapeutic especially when there are no strings attached, so go for it, girl! No one has to know." Chrissy winked.

"Are you serious Chrissy? Sophie exclaimed. "This is not what she needs right now! How can she have sex with him without feelings getting in the way? They share so much history together! Plus, if she gives in to this, she'll be cheating on Adam *again!*"

"Oh, stop being such a buzz kill, everything doesn't have to be so complicated! Sometimes it's ok to just go with the flow, enjoy it and not sit there and get all emotional about something, everything doesn't need to be analysed and thought over a hundred times, we are young, let us live grandma!" Chrissy yelled.

"Um guys, I really appreciate you giving me advice, but I think I need to decide for myself, and I think I should go. So please don't get worked up over this. We are here to enjoy, don't let this setback come in the way; and please don't get mad at each other over a pointless debate because of me," Anna requested.

The three girls looked at each other, "Oh alright I'm sorry I lost my cool Chris," Sophie said. "It's ok grandma, you know I still love you," Chrissy joked. Sophie shot her a sarcastic look and gave her a hug.

Anna smiled; she really didn't want her problems to frustrate her friends. They both advised her to be careful and to get back soon. Though later on, once Sophie had stepped out of the room, Chrissy pulled out a condom from her purse and gave it to Anna and said, "Just fun, no feelings," and then, with a cheeky smile she walked away. Anna really wished she could adopt Chrissy's attitude, this carefree approach towards sex would save her from getting hurt, but no, she needed to hear the 'I love you'; otherwise she could never sleep with a guy, that's why she never had one-night-stands and random hook-ups. She needed the safety and the love of relationships and yet she couldn't stay committed. Sometimes she wondered what was wrong with her!

But she didn't have time to analyse herself at that moment. She needed to get dressed, and get this over with. She got ready and took one last look at her reflection, she seldom liked what she saw but tonight was one of those rare occasions when she felt she looked nice. She smiled and grabbed her purse.

Dan was dropping her off in a cab but he didn't speak to her the entire way because he was disappointed in her. After the way Mike had judged her in anger and hurled those abuses at her two years back, she should have known better! It didn't matter that he was angry or drunk. You just don't treat another human being like that… period. But as usual Anna would never see that; she would just forgive and forget everything and let guys walk all over her.

Why couldn't she see how much *he* loved her and how much he could take care of her? Adam was a good guy he knew, but Anna didn't love him, she had just gotten used to him being around. But Dan could make her happy, truly very happy if she'd only give him a chance. He decided after she returned, he would have a little surprise waiting for her, just to make her happy and let her know that he was there for her. But for now, he decided to stay quiet.

Anna knew Dan had a lot to say, but she didn't want to ask him anything because she knew what he was going to say. So, she too simply kept quiet. They both shared the silence knowing fully well what the other was thinking. Finally, the cab pulled up at Palm Avenue and Anna felt her heart racing. She wanted to remain in the safety of the cab but she knew she had to get out and face Mike. She looked over at Dan, he gave her a quick hug and said, "Be careful." She nodded and stepped inside the restaurant. It was a stunning site. The whole place was lit up against the backdrop of the setting sun, sending a kaleidoscope of colours across the evening sky. Her admiration soon turned to nervousness as she spotted Mike sitting in one of the private dining areas at a candle lit table that was set up on a wooden panel floating on water. Damn! This place was romantic! How was she going to break it off in this dream like setting?

He got himself up from his chair, and held out his hand for her to take and walk across the two tiles on the water that lead to their private dining area in the pool. He looked so good in his suit, she was so glad she had gone for her LBD with a chic jacket and heels rather than jeans and a lacy top because this place was meant to host people dressed to the nines.

The panic set in from the time he hugged her, she couldn't make much eye contact again till the Merlot made its way to the table and she had had a glass or two. She loved the way his eyes were watching her and the compliments he showered on her. By the time the main course arrived she had already begun explaining her reasons for why nothing could happen between them tonight or anytime else, though she left Adam out of it. But the way he was looking at her with a sly smile on his face made her blush and she wasn't sure if he was even taking her seriously.

He tried to reason with her, and her mind did waver a bit here and there but she tried her best to stand her ground. Finally, the desserts arrived, but even the delightful treats could not save the crushing disappointment they both felt. After a bitter sweet ending they left the restaurant in different cabs. He had offered to drop her to the hotel but she knew if she got into that vehicle something would have surely happened so she promised him she would message him on reaching the hotel and gave him a quick goodbye kiss.

This was good; she didn't cave in and she did what she wanted to, so why did she feel this heavy weight of sadness pressing down on her? It was making her chest feel tight and before she knew it, tears were rolling down her face. She wanted him... or was it just her need to have someone to love her now that Adam wasn't around, that was making her weak? She wanted to turn the car around but she needed a sign, a sign to tell her she should go back to him.

She kept shuffling her playlist with the hope that it would land on one of 'their' songs so she could take that as a sign and rush back to him. Any excuse to get a sign from the universe so she could be with him... How pathetic was she? That's when she felt the cab stopping, but they weren't even half way to her hotel yet, she looked up and saw Mike peering at her through the window. She was too surprised to react at first but she quickly opened the door and got out.

She paid her cab driver and apologized for cutting the trip short. A slight drizzle had just started moistening the surroundings just like her heart. Mike took her in his arms and kissed her passionately, this kiss in the rain was the most amazing kiss of her life, she had never been kissed like that before, all she wanted was to stay there frozen forever in time. This was her sign; she took Mike's hand, he lead her into his cab and they headed for his hotel.

Chapter 8

Mike

The night seemed like a dream, he had her in his arms all night after they made love and though she was right there with him he just couldn't sleep a wink all night. He watched her naked body toss and turn under the sheets. Sometimes the sheet would slip off and he would catch a glimpse of her beautiful body just gleaming in the moonlight streaming in from the window.

Somewhere around dawn he fell asleep and was woken up to the sound of Anna's cell phone ringing incessantly around noon. That's when he knew the dream was over and that reality would soon set in. Anna groggily picked up the phone, it was some guy named Adam calling. He could hear Anna apologizing over and over again; why was this always the case with her; there was always some guy in the picture, why did she have to complicate things?

She ended the call looking a little hassled or was it guilty? He never could tell what she was thinking or feeling. Did he really want to sign up for this? Again? She coyly sat up on the bed wearing his shirt, she looked so sexy in it.

She said she had to leave because she had plans with her friends for the day and she was already late. He told her to ditch the gang and spend the day with him instead but she seemed hesitant. She said this trip was supposed to be a getaway with her friends. And this was an unexpected turn of events; she couldn't disappoint them by spending the last few days with him.

She was completely ruining his mood, he wanted her all to himself but clearly, that wasn't going to happen and if he insisted on coming along with her friends, he would look too clingy and that just wasn't him. Anna was on the phone again.

She came back looking a little exasperated and said that she had to leave and asked if he'd like to join her and her friends. He denied at first but she kept insisting so he agreed, though he had a feeling her friend Dan, in particular, wasn't going to be too thrilled about him tagging along, but he didn't care, he would get to spend more time with Anna and he was happy with that.

Since Anna had missed her morning plans with her friends and it was already noon, and the evening get together was not for a couple of hours, Mike suggested they hang back in the room have a late lunch, spend some alone time together before heading out, and luckily for him, Anna agreed. So, he pulled her back into bed and began undressing her.

Chapter 9

ANNA

Anna had messed up royally, she disappointed her friends especially Dan who it turns out, had planned a little surprise for her at the hotel the previous night because he knew she would be sad, having let Mike go. And she had completely forgotten about Adam, he was extremely worried about her; after having called her phone several times and gotten no answer he had called Sophie who covered for Anna and had told him that Anna had had a little too much to drink and had passed out. When he finally got through to her cell in the afternoon, Anna had apologized to him for drinking too much and not being able to talk. He was so trusting that he wasn't even angry that she didn't pick up his calls. He was just worried about her and wanted to know if she was ok, and yet again, he just believed the lies she fed him. She wondered if Mike would ever be this understanding.

She had lost count of the number of times they had made love since the previous night. She had slipped into a nap sometime around late afternoon. It was almost evening now; the sun had begun setting and the sky was streaked with saffron rays which flooded into their bedroom waking Anna from her sleep.

She felt Mike move beside her, he came closer and buried his face in her hair and took a big long whiff while caressing her, they made love again until they were both left breathless; their bodies bursting with pleasure.

For Anna it was always about a primal feeling with Mike. She loved his dominance, holding power over her, why did she like this? In the world of women empowerment, why did she want to be suppressed; submissive; was this normal? Maybe this was the reason Adam never stood a chance because he was the good guy, the sweet, caring, loving guy who didn't hold that kind of power over her and then there was Mike with his big strong features and his powerful persona that drew Anna to him effortlessly.

Why didn't the good guys win for a change, the soft and sensitive kind? Why was it that the bad guys were the ones girls couldn't resist?

Mike was always making inappropriate chauvinistic statements and passing them off as jokes. But somewhere deep down, Anna always felt that a part of him wanted to go back to a time when patriarchy was at its peak. Anna had always told him how she didn't appreciate his statements, but she was never stern enough and usually let it go in the end. She was sure if it was any other woman, she would have set him straight. Though there were times when Anna had retorted back in anger, he had always made it clear to her, that no other person, especially a woman had ever dared to speak to him that way!

He even told her that if he had as many relationships as her, it would be fine because he was a guy, but for a girl to have been with so many guys was wrong. And if he had a daughter, he would want her to have maybe one relationship, nothing more, and then get married.

He had a lot of good in him, his intelligence, his strength - both physically and mentally, but there were times she couldn't help but feel the narcissism come through in his actions and his over-confident and egoistic words. Anna didn't like this one bit especially; when he would talk down to her if she didn't know something or didn't agree with his views. Though his IQ was high, his EQ was almost non-existent. She often felt a lack of any empathy or understanding or even respect towards her. Everything about her was an issue: her voice, her over-sensitive reactions, her messiness, her general knowledge about things – everything.

He spoke to her rudely and said whatever came to his mind when he was angry. That horrible tone in his voice always made her want to curl up and die. While she, on the other hand, was always told to keep her voice down and not get angry!

At times, even if he wasn't angry he would belittle her. If she didn't hum a tune properly, if she said the name of the wrong ocean between two continents, or if she paused and stuttered while talking when recalling an event from memory (saying ummm.. ahhh while talking to a friend while trying to remember something was not a big deal, but to Mike it was unacceptable). This made Anna feel like she was always walking on eggshells around him, wondering what harmless conversation or even a word could set him off.

She could never meet his standards, because they were so high, they were out of reach.

And when she tried telling him to change this quality of his, to be kinder and more empathetic, he told her, he was tired of her repeating the same thing, and how earlier she would make him feel good about himself – the main reason he had loved her all this time. But now, he did not feel the same way anymore! So Anna apologized in fear of losing his love and accepted his nasty ways.

Her friends only knew a small fragment of how Mike had treated her over the years but, there was a lot they didn't know. There were things Anna had never told anyone about Mike because she was ashamed. There was a time, where for two-in-a-half years, Anna dated Mike. It was long-distance, but they managed to meet every couple of months and stay together for three or four months until he had to leave again. During this time, for the first time, despite the distance, Anna never cheated. She loved him truly and couldn't bring herself to be with anyone else. It was during this time she saw the worst of him. On several occasions in anger, he had cursed her and called her names that she would never forget. He had hit her several times and left behind bruises and cuts.

Mike had never missed an opportunity to bring her down regarding her work and her skills. But it didn't stop just with that; he would constantly criticize her for being an idiot, stupid, dumb. From her personality to her looks to the very fabric of her being, he would bring her down and criticize her constantly. This would be followed by periods of remorse and him making it up to her by being on his best behaviour and love bombing her. He would start to cry and beg her to stay saying he'd change and never behave like this again. But this wouldn't last, he would be abusive again and the cycle would repeat.

She often wondered during this time if he disliked everything about her why, didn't he just leave? The better question to be asked here is why didn't she leave? He was emotionally and physically abusing her, but she didn't have the strength to leave. She still stayed with him and continued to be disrespected until finally, she told him off in anger one night and cut off all contact with him. She had managed to maintain that stance for the last two years, till a few months ago, when he reconnected with her and she, as usual, seemed to have forgiven and forgotten everything!

For someone who always had self-esteem issues, this relationship did a number on her. She remembered Jake once warning her about Mike. When tensions started arising between the three of them, Jake had told her to stay away from Mike, that he wasn't a good person and was very disrespectful towards women. But of course, Anna didn't listen to him. She wished so many times over the years, she could tell Jake that he was right and she was sorry for not having listened to him and sorry for hurting him. But she never got to tell him this before he died. The pain and guilt she carried about Jake would haunt her for the rest of her life.

But then, knowing all this, why was she still in Mike's bedroom? Why was she still giving herself to him over and over again? He had belittled her, terribly! What was she doing? Was she ever going to learn?

Anna suddenly felt sick. She needed to get out of there. Sweet, trusting, Adam came into her mind and she was trying to choke back tears. She rushed into the loo and turned on the shower so Mike wouldn't hear her crying. But then again people change, he did explain his actions and aplogized many times. God why was this so confusing? Her confusions were cleared when Mike knocked on the door to come inside, one look at him and Anna melted into a pool of indecisions again inviting him in with open arms!

Chapter 10

MIKE

Mike was completely hooked again, hooked on her love, the way her lips curled into a smile, the way her body moved, her smell, her touch, her everything. He was in deep but he feared that he would be let down. She had an issue with lying but she had promised him she wouldn't lie this time around; he just had to wait and see.

He decided to try to stop his mind from wandering as he got ready. They finally left the hotel room and met up with her friends, who weren't too excited to see him, well Dan anyway, the girls seemed fine. He could sense a lot of hostility from Dan but he decided to let it slip, because, how did it even matter? Mike was sure he had a crush on Anna, but then, who didn't? And he had her, not him, so he decided not to let Dan get under his skin.

They were all having a good time and decided to head to Cavalli Club. Everyone was drinking and dancing. Mike was all over Anna on the dance floor and he could see Dan from the corner of his eye watching them, but he didn't mind he just kept on dancing with Anna. It wasn't until he whispered in her ear, "You're coming back to my place tonight, right? Because I leave in a few days and we need to figure out what we are going to do about us."

It was then that Anna stopped dancing and looked him in the eye with that familiar look he knew too well; that unsure, grieving look. She took his hand and led him outside where it was a little quieter. She said, "I am actually with someone back home, his name is Adam, he's my best friend, the most wonderful friend I've ever had and I'm not sure what to do."

He knew it! "But just last night you said you loved me!" Mike protested.

"I had had a lot to drink plus all the sex made me feel so close to you. I got swept away by the emotions, the hormones and being drunk didn't help either. I'm so sorry Mike," Anna said, not without regret.

He knew it… he knew she would do this. He wondered why he had gotten his hopes up again. He had been through the same thing enough times, so why was he foolish enough to get swept up by her words again? When was he ever going to learn that no matter how strong his feelings were towards Anna, they were not meant to be together?

"What's the point of saying sorry, don't say it, I knew you'd hurt me again and I just let you, I always let you… why do you do this to me every time Anna? Why?" Mike asked in frustration.

"I'm sorry Mike I really am, it's not that I don't want to be with you, it's just too complicated right now." Anna replied.

"It's always complicated with you isn't it, Anna?" Mike snarled.

"Don't do that ok, you are not perfect you know! I still haven't been able to get over how horrible you were to me the time we were together!

Most girls would have never spoken to you again after how you behaved! Also, even before anything happened between us last night, I think I had made it very clear to you that we couldn't be together. I might not have mentioned Adam, but that was my choice! So when you chased me down in your cab, you should not have got your hopes up about anything long term!" Anna was now screaming and caught the attention of people around. She was also surprised at herself for being able to retort back, perhaps for the first time!

"People are watching us, keep your voice down! Stop bringing up the past. Why do women always do this? You need to let it go and not bring it up each time we have a fight; it just shows how weak and pathetic you are…" Mike said.

Mike could see Anna was furious and he had set her off but he was really mad at her too. "Don't ask me to keep my voice down I will yell and scream all I want! I will also never forget all the things you did and said to me *ever*! Why can't you just understand I need time? Things happened but I'm not ready for a relationship… especially a long-distance one!" Anna cried.

"You will never be ready for a long-distance relationship Anna, you are just too weak and worthless, always needing someone to be there for you. Why can't you be strong? It's so pathetic needing someone all the time! You will always need a guy; you can't live without a guy to love you and hold you and yeah most importantly fuck you!" Mike said disgustedly.

He immediately wanted to take back his words because he knew he had taken it too far yet again, but it was too late. "How dare you? I knew it! I knew you haven't changed a bit, you're still the same piece of shit I always knew. Well, fuck you!" Anna yelled and started to storm away. Mike needed a time out so he let her walk away. He wanted to have a smoke, cool down and then go inside to talk to her again calmly; so he lit his cigarette.

He had just taken his first drag, when he felt someone push him hard from behind. He was a big guy, and it wasn't easy to get him down. He just felt a little nudge and turned around to see Dan looking acidly at him. Was this little bugger really trying to fight him? He appreciated his attempt, he really did, but he knew he wasn't going down.

"All you ever do is hurt her, I never liked you from the beginning, you made her cry again, I warned her, I told her you hadn't changed but she didn't listen. But I knew you'd show your true colours in time. Now you better stay away from her or else…" Dan slurred.

Mike let out a laugh, Dan had clearly had a little too much to drink; he couldn't even stand straight and was barely able to frame his sentences. He decided not to waste his energy on this, he smirked and was just about to look away when Dan's fist came swinging at him, Mike moved, Dan swung again and missed, but he wasn't giving up, he pushed Mike really hard this time and that's when Mike had enough, he gave Dan one big push and Dan fell into the ditch they were standing close too.

Few people nearby had gathered to see what was happening and Anna and her friends had clearly seen what had happened on their way out and immediately rushed over. He didn't want to do this, he really didn't, but Dan had left him no choice.

Chapter 11

ANNA

"What did you do Mike?!" Anna yelled. But all Mike had to say was Dan started it. Chrissy had left some time ago with a guy she had met staying at the Hyatt, so it was just her and Sophie there to help Dan, he was hurt and bruised. They pulled a shocked and a very drunk Dan out of the ditch and into a cab while Anna looked Mike in the eye one last time to say, "How many times are we going to do this until it finally sets in that we are never going to be together? I'm tired of this, so please Mike, let this go; we are just not meant to be!"

Anna turned around and stepped into the cab with her friends, as the cab pulled away, she saw Mike standing there, helpless, hopeless… for the first time he didn't look so strong to her, he just looked like an ordinary guy who had had his heart broken. She wiped her tears and looked away. She still had no idea about what she truly wanted. But right now, she needed to give her thoughts a rest and be there for her friend.

By the time they got back to the hotel and got Dan to shower and head to bed, it was 1:45 am. She checked her phone there were no calls from Mike; well, why would there be? Anna wondered what he was thinking... what he was feeling. Sophie broke her thoughts, "Hey, how are you holding up?" She gave her a hug. "You know I love you, and I don't want to say this, but I told you not to go, this would not end well, it never does with him. Why do you do this to yourself Anna? I've seen you for years now, you're not able to break this toxic pattern with him and you always end up hurting yourself, him and whoever else you're seeing. I didn't come here to lecture you, I'm sorry… let's talk about this tomorrow maybe… but only if you want to. And don't worry, I'm sure he'll call, he always does." But Anna was doubtful, too much had happened since high school and maybe it was really over this time around.

"What about Chris? Is she ok?" Anna asked. "Ya, I just spoke to her. She said she is safe and will be back tomorrow morning," Sophie said. "Ok, thanks Soph, I love you," Anna hugged Sophie and wished her a goodnight. Soph's hugs were the best, they always made Anna feel like everything was going to be alright. But tonight, even Soph's hug was not enough to make Anna feel better. She lay awake for the rest of the night wondering if Mike was thinking of her all alone in his room, or whether he had hooked up with one of his slinky co-workers instead, he surely didn't waste much time if that was the case. Anna decided to not have these unkind thoughts and tried to calm her mind so she could fall asleep, but she wasn't able to turn her thoughts off. Sometime during day-break Anna finally slipped into an unrestful sleep.

After a few hours Anna awakened to the sunlight streaming in through her window, she was not ready to face the day yet, but no matter how much she tried to fall back asleep, she just couldn't, her mind was racing with too many thoughts. She checked her phone to see if there were any calls or messages from Mike; there weren't. Instead, there was a warm good morning message from Adam. Sweet, loving, unsuspecting

Adam… how she had let him down, again. She sighed and pulled off the covers and went outside to meet her friends.

At 10 am, it was still quite early for Anna. She found Dan standing in the balcony looking out at the spectacular view of the city's skyline. She inched closer him, "How are you feeling?" she asked.

"Fine," came a curt answer.

"You didn't need to do that you know, I appreciate the gesture, it was really sweet of you to stand up for me, but you know how strong he is and in the end you are the one who got hurt, you could have saved yourself the pain and humiliation, it just wasn't worth it don't you think?"

Dan turned around to look at her and she could see the anger in his eyes. He spoke with resentment, "You can't even console me without making it clear that he is bigger and better than me, can you? I did this for you Anna; I stood up to that bully who never treated you right. Someone needed to show him his place. I failed… but at least I tried! But you have no idea how small you made me feel right now by saying what you just did." His voice had softened now and the anger in his eyes had been taken over by grief.

"I didn't mean it like that Dan, I'm so sorry, I didn't mean to bring you down. I appreciate you doing this for me; I just meant you didn't need to go through all the trouble of doing this. I'm sorry it just came out all wrong, I'm really sorry." Anna grabbed on to his arm and placed her head lightly on his shoulder. They stood there like that for a while, neither saying a word. Minutes went by until Dan took his hand away from

Anna's and took her in his arms and kissed her forehead. Anna knew then, they were good. That's the thing with friendships, the cuts were always so easily mended with a simple Band-Aid, but relationships, the wounds ran so deep and got so messy that no tourniquet was strong enough to stop the blood and pain.

While walking back to the foyer Dan whispered in Anna's ears, "I love you, Anna, I've loved you for six years now, when will it be my chance?" And just like that, the sanity and peace of the friendship was ruined at that moment, the second the 'L' word was whispered, all gone. Before Anna could answer, Dan said, "Don't say anything now, just come out with me one night while we are still here, just one date, and if I don't sweep you off your feet and if you feel nothing, I will gracefully step back and dutifully fulfil the role of the lovable friend, I promise. So, what do you say? Give me one chance, please?"

How could she say no to that goofy grin! But, she had been telling him for six years now that she wasn't interested, she even went along with his 'give me a chance to sweep you off your feet dates' but nothing happened and she told him to back off, which he did do for a while but again it was back to square one. "You sure if I feel nothing this time you will let this go because this has gone on for too long and you need to move on and find someone who can truly love you the way you deserve to be loved."

"I promise," came his sincere answer. Anna took a deep breath and agreed, she hoped after this date she wouldn't end up losing a great friend.

Chapter 12

DAN

She agreed one more time, one more time she had given him a chance, he couldn't blow it now, not this time; he had to do something extravagant, something extreme to show her that he was the one; he was the one for her. She was at her most vulnerable state right now, he knew Mike would slip up, misogynistic men like that always do, yet girls always fall for them. How unfair was that? It forced guys like him to settle for the role of the best friend, never getting the girl but always watching her hurt herself, over and over again… Dan wondered if the sweet, loving guy ever won this battle? Or did the alpha male always take the lead?

He knew he had to up his game before she changed her mind or before Mike salvaged the situation and weaseled his way back in. Google would have to save him at this point, the best place, the best time, the best transport to get there, he had to plan it all, there was no time to waste; he also had to find the perfect gift, to blow her away.

He opened his laptop and got to work. After a few hours, he narrowed down a couple of places. His stomach grumbled and he decided to grab a bite to eat. The girls were down by the poolside and Anna had been holed up in her room ever since the episode with Mike. Even Chris's positive, upbeat vibes were not enough to make Anna feel any better this time. She tried a lot to entice Anna with new places to visit and things to do, Soph tried too but nothing worked. They decided to let Anna be on her own for a while to give her some time and space to feel better. He knocked on her door, and saw her curled up in bed with a bottle of whiskey by her side, miserable. He wanted to reach out and hold her, take care of her, instead he said to her, "Anna you've been drinking on an empty stomach, you really should eat something, I'm going down to grab a bite to eat. You want me to get you something? Or I can just stay here and we can order room service." he said.

"No, "Anna sighed. He didn't ask again because he knew it was pointless. He made his way downstairs and ordered himself a big juicy steak with a side of veggies and mashed potatoes. He wolfed down the steak to satisfy his grumbling tummy. After the meal, he decided to take a little something for Anna. He knew what she'd like, something meaty to start with and end with something sweet and chocolaty.

He went upstairs opened the door, came in and placed the food on the bed, very close to Anna's nose. She kept her eyes closed, but sniffed the aroma, but she turned the other way. Stubborn girl. She knew she was starving, so why did she have to keep up this drama, that too for a loser like Mike. Dan waited a little longer hoping she would turn and give in. A few moments passed, she shuffled around and finally sighed, turned around, gave Dan an annoyed look and tore open the parcel to devour the double meat BBQ steak. She didn't stop there, after that she went for the Mississippi Mud pie and the Red Velvet Jar. Finally looking satisfied she looked up at Dan a little embarrassed, but a lot happier than she had been in a while. She thanked him and went to the washroom to clean up, Dan had to help her all the way because she was drunk and couldn't walk straight. He tried to tuck her back into bed but she kept on rambling about Mike and Adam and something about work and her boss, she was slurring so much, Dan couldn't make out what she was saying, but whatever it was, was making her really upset. She started bawling and was shaking uncontrollably. He hated seeing her like this. He held her in his arms, rocked her back and forth while stroking her hair and assuring her everything was going to be alright and he was right there; within minutes she passed out.

He kissed her forehead and quietly slipped out of the room. He decided to let her wallow in bed for another day, but tomorrow night he was putting his plan into action and getting the girl of his dreams to fall in love with him.

Chapter 13

ANNA

Everything was dark, why was everything so dark? Anna couldn't see anything… she feared the dark, the blackness surrounding her was closing in on her. Anything sinister could happen here, anything evil could harm her, she had to get out, but she couldn't see anything. She stretched her hand out to feel if anything was around her, she felt nothing, she called out, "Hello is anybody there; can anyone hear me?" No response.

She had to get out of there, she had to try; she couldn't be trapped in this dark nothingness forever. She inched forward, one step, two steps, three, four, five, she was just about to take the next step, but she felt something pull her back, she turned around but there was nothing there. She felt a chill up her spine, but she brushed it off and moved forward again. She made it a couple more steps forward and felt something pulling her back again, a force gripping her tight, not letting her move forward. Despite this, she kept going but every couple of steps she would feel that force pulling her back, again and again but Anna didn't give up…

This went on for some time. Anna was unaware of how many hours had passed… She was tired, frustrated, the tears were almost about to spill from her eyes. She let out a loud cry and started sobbing. She was never going to make it, her whole body ached, she wanted to sit down, she wanted to get rid of this weight holding her back. She was beginning to give up; succumb to her fate when suddenly she heard someone laughing, she listened intently, it was a child's laughter, a little girl, she sounded so happy, so full of joy with not a care in the world.

That sweet laughter felt like music to Anna's ears, she needed to know who this little girl was, this meant that she was not alone here, there was some else here! A little kid, but that was enough, all she needed was someone, so she wouldn't feel so scared and alone all by herself engulfed in this darkness. She wiped her tears, got up on her feet and fought the force holding her back.

With each step she fought a little harder, the force got stronger but she kept fighting harder, the pain shot up her legs, her back, and the tears kept coming, but she didn't give up. The laughter of the little girl got louder and louder and she knew she was close, very close to finding her.

Finally, she saw a glimmer of light in the distance and as she inched closer and closer, the silhouette of a house came into the frame, a big green park, blue skies, and a cobbled street, this looked very familiar. As Anna got closer it hit her, this big beautiful yellow house with the large glass windows was her house! Her childhood home in Kolkata! The big green park came into full view, she loved this park, especially during *Durga Puja* – a beautiful *pandal* would be constructed and the giant idols of *Maa Durga* and all her children would be placed inside the gorgeous setup. This would be their home for five days, during which a series of rituals would take place with flowers and fire, hymns and *prasad*. The whole city would light up.

At the end of the fifth day, when the celebrations were over, the idols would be immersed in the river and the *pandal* brought down. That is when Anna and her friends, some from her neighbourhood but mostly children from the nearby slums would go into the park after sunset, when it was dark and search for the glistening golden specks which had fallen off from the idols' clothes and jewellery. They would lay hidden among the grass for the kids to find. This little treasure hunt was something Anna used to look forward to every year before they had to move again to another city. She hated moving; as she had lived in many houses across many cities. As her dad's business flourished, they kept moving on to bigger and better places, but she could never call any place her home, except this house. This was her favourite place, the one house where she truly felt at home.

As Anna got even closer, she finally caught a glimpse of the little girl. She let out a gasp when she realized that the little girl was *her*! It was Anna back when she was a kid. Little Anna was wearing a pretty red dress, frolicking about in her garden, humming a tune, skipping and dancing around, laughing and playing with the three kittens her nanny had rescued. She was waiting for the sun to set to begin the hunt. She looked so happy, all by herself, she didn't need anyone else, she didn't care about the world around her or what they thought of her. She didn't care if she looked fat or thin, or if the dress looked good on her, she didn't need anyone else, especially not a guy to make her happy, she was content and carefree with herself, living in the moment, enjoying it.

Seeing this brought more tears to Anna's eyes, all she wanted to do was jump in to play with little Anna, hug her real tight and ask her, "Where had you been all this time? I missed you,

I'm so sorry I forgot you, I love you so much, you made me so happy… I want it all back…your innocence, your happiness… I want *you* back!" She wanted to play with her, go on that hunt with her again and feel free, oh so free from all the burdens, mistakes and regrets of her grown-up life!

Anna ran towards the little girl away from the darkness and tried to leap into the frame but something caught her mid-way, it was that earlier force again, stronger than ever. It wrapped around her waist real tight and pulled her back. She tried to free herself, but the force was too strong. It kept pulling her further and further away from little Anna. "No! Please let me go!" Anna screamed and begged, but the force kept pulling her away. It was engulfing her back into the darkness, till she couldn't see little Anna anymore, she couldn't hear her laughter; everything was turning cold again; sinister...

She turned around to look at the force once again and this time it showed itself, and, Anna couldn't believe her eyes, the force too was her! Only this time she was older maybe sixteen, but wait she saw another *her*, this time eighteen, and they kept multiplying, all of them were Anna at different stages in her life, twelve, fifteen, nineteen, twenty-one, twenty-five, twenty-six, and there she was the actual twenty-eight years old Anna, caught in this web of all her former selves, the selves which made all the mistakes, had all the regrets… dragging her away from her true self, her real happy self.

The more she struggled to get away, the more they all pulled her towards them until she got sucked into a deep, unfathomable darkness.

Chapter 14

ANNA

Anna's eyes jolted open; she sprung up from her bed, drenched in sweat breathing heavily. *It was a dream, just a dream; no, an alcohol-induced nightmare brought on by the contents of the half bottle of whiskey you emptied right up to the last drop along with your fragile state of mind and emotions,* she consoled herself trying to calm herself down and normalise her breathing. She looked at her phone it was 3 am. Her first instinct was to jump out of bed and rush to her friend's room. She even got up to do so, but something deep inside told her to not be such a coward anymore, and face this situation herself. She would have to stop expecting somone to be around all the time and learn to deal with things herself at some point of time in her life. At twenty-eight, perhaps this was as good a time to start, as any!

She grabbed a drink of water and laid back down, this time, fully awake. What had that dream meant? She was not one to interpret dreams but this one really struck a chord and she wasn't able to shake the feeling the dream had left behind. She opened Google to find out more about dream meanings, but she couldn't find anything pertaining to her dream, so she closed the tab and decided to let this go and try to fall back asleep.

She closed her eyes, tossed and turned for about an hour or two, she tried thinking of her special date with Dan, Adam, Mike, sheep, flowers, and a whole host of random things, but nothing worked. She looked at her phone again, 5:30 am. Should she wake one of her friends? She just needed one, actually anyone to fill the loneliness.

Wait! Was her mind, rather her subconscious trying to tell her something through this dream? But what? There were so many versions of her in the dream that it was strange and scary. She realised that there were so many parts of her, that together made her who she was today, some flawed, some disastrous and some, though few, at peace and happy.

It was now 6:30 am. Anna knew there was no point in trying to sleep anymore. She got up and drew back the curtains; the dark sky was slowly turning to light to bring forth the beginning of a new day. Anna had never seen the sunrise before, it was a magnificent sight indeed – the sun peeking out from the horizon, the speckled hues of yellow and orange beginning to paint the sky, an aura of harmony and peace all around… Anna took it all in; the beauty of the universe, the freshness of a new day, the re-birth… Anna closed her eyes and took in a long and deep breath to allow all of it to soak in. It was a new experience for her.

She then slowly opened her eyes, and suddenly, things began to make sense to her…she understood everything!

Chapter 15

DAN

Everything was set, today was the day he was going to make Anna fall in love with him. He had checked and re-checked; paid attention to every tiny detail to make sure everything would be perfect for her. This was big, he had never done this for anyone in his life, but he knew she was worth it. Was he crazy to do this? What if after all this effort she still wouldn't feel anything for him?

He loved the time when Anna had just come out of that awful relationship with the guy who used to beat her up, and yet she still stayed with him… He often wondered why she stayed. After he finally left, she was desperate to move on and get over him, and that was the time he had told her that he liked her. She was hesitant at first but had then decided to give him a shot.

He loved those few months where he had Anna all to himself. They would sit and talk over coffee for hours, head out to the park and chat, she would come over and have a couple of drinks with him, they'd kiss and he'd feel like he was on top of the world.

What changed? What made her go away from him? As usual, there were a line of guys after her, and she simply moved away from him. He knew she was still healing from her recent breakup and was confused and it's not like they were a real couple.

She told him many times that she was in a bad place; all confused and that is why she leaned on him for support, but she never really felt that way about him, there was no romantic feeling that she ever had for him, and this broke his heart, but he understood and agreed to be her friend, as long he didn't lose her. When she started dating Adam he knew that she didn't love Adam either, just like his real name suggested, he had simply become a 'habit' for her, she felt familiar and comfortable with him, and so, despite her being with him, over the years, Dan kept trying to win her back but failed... each and every time.

He decided to let these feeling go. He knew he had pulled all the stops and she would be blown away. This had to be it. Things between them were left unfinished; he really wanted her, but she kept giving herself to other guys, never him... why didn't she choose him?

No! He wasn't going to be disheartened. He looked at the time. 3 pm. Anna still hadn't stepped out of her room yet. She knew she had her date with him that evening; *she better not be in bed crying again,* he thought. All this while, he had given her time to mourn, but now, it was his chance.

He knocked on her door, but there was no answer, so he slowly opened the door. No Anna. The bed had been slept in but there seemed to be no one around. He checked the washroom, still no Anna. Then he noticed all her stuff was gone! No clothes were thrown around the room, no shoes on the floor, and no suitcase either!

He felt a sudden surge of panic rise within him! Where was she?

Chapter 16

ANNA

Anna's phone rang; Dan calling. She had a couple of missed calls from him and her girlfriends but she wasn't ready to talk to them yet. There was an announcement, her flight was boarding; she got up and stood in the queue. This was the right thing to do, she was going home and she was going to make things right.

She had left Dan hanging, but honestly, she knew that even if this date had been right out of a romance novel, she still wouldn't feel that way about him. So, there was really no point in wasting his time or hers, especially hers. She had wasted too much time letting her emotions take the reins; it was time for her mind to take charge of her life.

Why had it taken her this long to figure things out? All that suffering, all that pain, for what? It was such a waste! Or was it? Because it finally led her to this moment of realization!

But were the beatings, the abuses; the sexual assault she had endured, all worth the realization now? Yes! Of course. Because this could stop her from ending up in similar situations in the future. She still had her entire life ahead of her and she was going to make these coming chapters some of her best.

She thought to herself and realized she had never had any self-love, self-respect, self-confidence or self-esteem; all she had were her insecurities. She wondered how she ended up this way.

Seeking help was now something she had to do, and she knew it. She realised that she was a troubled individual with no sense of self and a crazy need to be loved. It was like her drug, a bad habit she needed to kick before it ruined her completely.

She had to find that little girl again, the girl who didn't need any validation or love from anyone else but herself, who was not afraid to say 'no' when situations called for it, she didn't need to please anyone else, all she needed was herself and that was enough; being herself was enough.

Tears of regret, sorrow and hope streamed down Anna's face. She was now seated inside her flight, about to make a journey to set things right. She knew the help had to be professional, and had decided to see a therapist to help her overcome these issues. She just needed a helping hand to guide her in the right direction.

The announcement to turn off all electronic gadgets was being repeated. Anna quickly took out her phone and left a message for her friends, *I'm sorry I left for back home. It was a spur of the moment decision, please don't be mad. It was something I had to do. I'm on the flight now about to take off, I'm fine now; I'm finally fine… thank you guys for everything. See you back home. Love you.* She sent the message off to everyone and switched off her phone with tears still rolling down her face. "You ok miss?" An elderly looking gentleman in the seat next to hers asked.

"Never been better," Anna answered with a big smile.

Chapter 17

Dan

Dan was furious! *How could she do this?* He thought to himself. All his planning went down the drain. The beautiful gift he bought for her was so expensive and he hoped that the store would take returns and refund him. She gave him hope and just like that took it all away, he had never been this mad at her before. What had happened to make her just up and leave?

Sophie and Chrissy weren't too pleased either, but they would get over it, after all, they hadn't spent a fortune on Anna. They still had two more days left and didn't want to change the tickets now, so they decided to stay. Though Soph was a little hesitant leaving Anna alone, but Chris convinced her that Anna would be fine, and they should enjoy their last two days and then they would go straight home to check on Anna, and in the meantime, they could be in touch with her over the phone to make sure she was ok.

Dan was determined to forget all about Anna and drink his weight in alcohol and try and hook up with someone with Chris being his wing woman; she was good at these things. All this time he had steered clear of other girls because of Anna, but now, he had decided to get over her no matter what it took.

As Dan was giving himself this little pep talk, he heard the doorbell ring. The girls were getting ready to step out so he went to get the door. He opened the door to Mike. One look at him and that little pep talk he was giving himself went right out the door. He couldn't let him have Anna, no way, she was meant to be with him!

"Is Anna here? I've been trying to call her, her phone's off, and her phone is never off, so I got a little concerned and wanted to talk, is she here?"

"Oh! Now you're concerned about Anna, is it?" Dan scoffed back.

"Is she here or not?!" Mike sneered.

"No she's not, she took an early flight out to Chicago today, all thanks to you, you ruined her trip, all she wanted was some alone time with her friends and you had to come in with your fake macho bravado and hurt her again!"

Mike smirked, turned around and walked away. Dan shrugged off the urge to punch him and instead slammed the door shut. Would Mike go after Anna? He couldn't let that happen, he needed to get to her first. He unlocked his phone to look for flight tickets.

Chapter 18

ANNA

After about thirteen hours Anna was finally in a cab on her way back home. She still hadn't switched on her phone; she wasn't ready to face the wrath of her friends, especially Dan. He must have been so disappointed. But she had to do this for herself. She was done doing things to please other people just so that they wouldn't get angry with her. She was always afraid, if they were mad at her, they would leave her, and she wasn't capable of being on her own… but not anymore.

She pressed down on the power button and sure enough, there were plenty of missed calls and messages; some from her girlfriends voicing their concern as well as their irritation, for having left them like that. Few were from Dan, a lengthy message about the wonderful plans he had for her and how disappointed he was. And then there was another one from him saying it was ok and he too was on his way back home and he had something for her. *Damn this boy never gives up* Anna thought. But this time she would have to be stern with him. No more letting him down easy, it had not worked in the past, hence she had to be a little harsh for the message to sink in this time.

Then she saw it, Mike's name, her heart started beating faster and her breathing got heavier. Just relax she told herself, *no*

matter what he says DO NOT go running back to him, not this time.
She clicked on the message:

Anna,

How can you be so cold? Do I not matter to you at all? You just walked away, left for back home without even saying goodbye. I thought you loved me enough to give me this much. It's always like this, you walk away, some time passes and I come after you, and there is no shame in that for me, but I don't know how we end up here every time. Why can't things just be peaceful for once? I have given up trying to understand you… you are so complicated I can't begin to make sense of what keeps going on in your head and your heart. Is there any room for me there at all, or is it truly over after eleven years?

I wish I could fly down to see you, but duty calls and I have to go. Look… I'll do whatever you want to do, ok? But just take your time, please think things over again and let me know your decision. Call me… I miss your voice; I'd love to hear your voice, even if you're scolding me.

Mike

Anna had to muster up all her strength to not call him back, right at that moment and fix everything and be his again. She decided to wait and think about what she wanted to say to him, she had to let him down gently even though she didn't want to. She had to do it… move away from him for good – he was not right for her… she too wasn't right for him. There were too many compatibility issues. Once the passion faded, there would be nothing left between them. There were too many differences in their values and ways of thinking. Plus, the pain of the emotional and physical abuse. It would never work out in the long run. They didn't even understand each other! Anna needed him to understand this, so they could both move on.

Finally, after Anna reached home, her mum was her usual uncaring self towards Anna's return, so she didn't expect much from her anyway. But her dad asked her about her trip and she briefly gave him some anecdotes. She went into her room and thought everything over again.

By the time she had freshened up, unpacked and eaten her dinner, it was midnight. She still wasn't tired. She thought about her whole life; the mistakes, the regrets, the pain and sorrow, the damage she had done to her body and her health. She looked at her reflection in the mirror, Aayena, the name that meant mirror, and yet she was never able to look at her reflection for more than a few seconds without feeling exposed, dirty and vulnerable. Why was that? Did she really hate herself that much? Tonight, she decided to face her reflection, look herself in the eye and feel every emotion that came her way. She cried... cried for hours. After that when she felt like she could breathe again, she drank a whole bottle of water, took a deep breath and started typing furiously.

She left messages for people she felt had wronged her. There was a special message for her boss who she had unblocked for the moment, and her ex who physically abused her... things she had wanted to say for a very long time, finally came pouring right out of her heart and it felt really good – kind of liberating. The flow continued... it was as if she had to say whatever she wanted to, to everyone she wanted to say them to, right then! There was the one who said he loved her and then left; there were a few who didn't seem to hear or understand her polite "No" and came on to her; it was a rather long list. After she had meticulously covered each and every person who had hurt or disturbed her in some way, she blocked them on every front and deleted their contacts from her phone. She also consciously decided to have her number changed soon.

Next came the people she had hurt, the sweet guys who didn't deserve any of it. She spoke from her heart and hoped they would understand.

Then came Dan, a strong-worded message was sent to him asking him to give up once and for all, because he had no chance with her. It was a bit rude, but it had to be done. She made it very clear, that she did not want him in her life as anything more than a friend; not in the past, not now, not ever! And, if after this, he didn't want to be friends, then that meant, he never was a good friend to begin with… Damn! Why didn't she have this clarity earlier? It could have saved her from a lot of unnecessary situations.

She then took out a photo frame of her and Jake, looking at his striking smile and twinkling eyes made her heart ache; oh, how she missed him, but she hoped he was happy wherever he was. She looked into his beautiful brown eyes and apologized to him, kissed his smiling face and held his picture to her heart for a while… until her tears stopped.

Finally, it was Mike's turn; this was the hardest to write. Through a fresh batch of tears, she wrote:

Mike

I'm not being cold. It's equally hard for me to keep away from you, but we are not good for each other and it's not just about the distance. The passion and pheromones take over and cloud my judgement when

I'm with you, but the reality is we are too different. We tried staying together and that turned out to be a disaster. When the passion fades you are just left with that one person for the rest of your life, the person whose flaws are real, but you don't care because you love them anyway. The passionate lover is replaced by the compassionate best friend who you want to be with for the rest of your life.

We were never friends; we were always caught up in the passion and intensity of it all. Trust me when I say this, I love you, a part of me always might because you were my first BIG LOVE, but we are not good for the long run, we are good for the short honeymoon phase and deep down inside even you know it.

I adore the man that you are Mike, but in you I found a lover not a friend. I think it's best for us, if we keep our distance for now and not be in touch till we are fully over each other, ok?

"With or without you ... with or without you... I can't live with or without you..." I'll always remember our song... seems more accurate now than ever, doesn't it...?

Goodbye Mike.

This was it; there was no going back now. The tears kept coming and Anna felt them all. There were no more backups now, she was all in with Adam. In her heart, she felt he truly was the one, the lover, the best friend – her world. He had his flaws but who didn't. And now that she thought about it, he was like her father in quite a few ways. And their relationship was a lot like her parents'. This realization made Anna smile because she loved how her parents were, their bond was always strong despite her mum's issues; they both balanced each other out – best friends and partners.

Adam was due back in two weeks, she decided that she would tell him everything that had happened recently. She also decided to tell him that she needed time for herself to be properly single. But he was truly the one she wanted to be with, and if he still wanted to, he could wait for her. She knew there was a chance, he would walk away after all she'd put him through in the past and now this, but she was willing to take the risk even if it meant losing him.

She gathered herself, stopped the tears, and finally sent one last message: *I love you…*

Chapter 19

ADAM

Adam woke up to his phone buzzing. There was a message from Anna, "I Love You," it read. A smile crept across his face. He replied with an "I love you too." He was going to see her in two weeks and he couldn't wait. His small trip back home had turned into a big family vacation with his parents and his siblings jetting off to Europe.

He was thrilled that he got to visit a lot of places: Paris, Amsterdam, Belgium. The food was great, but he missed his mom's home-cooked meals, he was a true Punjabi at heart; Butter Chicken and Naan were all he needed to keep him satisfied.

He wished Anna had come along on this vacation, she would have loved it here. He didn't understand why she was always worried about him cheating and falling in love with some other girl. The girls here were different no doubt, from the way they dressed to the way they spoke, but none of them came close to Anna. To him, Anna was the most beautiful girl in the world. Many times, guys say this to girls to make them feel better, but it was true in his case, he never looked twice at any girl.

He had more to be worried about with Anna, given her history, but he kept his cool and decided to trust her. The Dubai trip bothered him especially with Dan tagging along, but he knew she needed this, so he let her go and all seemed well, so he was hopeful when he returned, she wouldn't drop any bombs, since the nightmares were back, and he didn't think he could take any more pain.

He decided to not dwell on these thoughts any longer and got dressed to head out with his family for the day

Chapter 20

Anna

The two weeks that followed were a drag, not only was Anna bored out of her mind, but she was also getting quite lonely. She needed the attention and it was driving her mad. She had cut off from every man she had ever known. She had to force herself from unblocking Mike and talking to him because she was dying without him. She would leave herself little voice notes telling herself why she shouldn't reach out to Mike and focus on herself.

These voice notes helped. For the first time, she was being there for herself and not ringing her friends to guide her. Dan and she had a falling out, he was very hurt by her choosing not to give him another chance and running away, but she had to make him understand that she didn't want him in her life as a boyfriend, she just wanted the friendship. She decided to give him time and hoped he would eventually come around.

The only thing she looked forward to each week were the two days with the healer. She preferred the word healer over the word therapist because it felt more real. These sessions with Susan helped her understand herself better. The talking and the regression therapy, the one that delved into her childhood memories were especially insightful. She realised that most of the mistakes she had made in her life, or the issues she always had trouble with, had stemmed from her experiences in her childhood.

She was born to a bi-polar mother, who never wanted her and made that very clear through her actions. And her father, the one person she felt connected with and could count on, was never around due to his work and travels. He was a businessman and had to build his empire from scratch, his absence was always felt in their home. She didn't have any siblings to turn to either. Being sexually abused as a kid on more than one occasion, made things worse.

It was their trusted chauffeur who keep lifting her up and squeezing her chest till it hurt, and ran his hands up and down her leg, unzipped his pants to reveal what was underneath and asked her to do the same. She knew something was wrong, but she was just a kid at the time and didn't understand what was going on. So, she told her mum, but she never believed Anna, and her dad was never around.

She realized, despite all the happy times in her childhood, and she did have many to be thankful for, she never was close to her family. Yes, they went on vacations, but when it came to real things, there was no one there for her. She was not blaming anyone, she loved her parents and knew they did their best, but parenting is hard, and sometimes, without knowing it, parents can harm their kids.

In-utero rejection trauma is what Susan had mentioned. Anna wasn't aware of this concept, but she was told that the child is always able to feel the mother's emotions when it is in the womb. Anna had been an accidental pregnancy, her mother never wanted to have children. Anna was able to feel her mother's negative emotions towards her. The feeling of not being wanted and not being loved was something Anna had to cope with even before coming into this world.

Her parents were also planning for an abortion, but they weren't able to go through with it, because her mother was too far along in her pregnancy, her aunt had thoughtlessly mentioned this to Anna a long time ago. "Before you were born, your life was already at threat. You had to fight to survive in the womb. The need for love, and feeling wanted, became your way of survival," Susan told her.

Her father's absence due to his work, and travels and living away from them for a couple of years, made her seek this love from other men. She never thought of herself as someone having daddy issues, but clearly, she did. "You kept looking for the love your parents couldn't give you. And since you had to fight to survive in the womb, the need for love, approval, and being wanted, became your only way of survival, without which you felt like you would die," Susan shared.

And the trauma of sexual abuse she endured made matters worse. One of the many times she needed her parents, they were not there for her; they didn't believe her. She was always in the care of her nanny, who looked after her through her formative years.

No wonder she was never close to her parents. And her escape was always with her friends and through her relationships. No wonder it was so hard for her to say no with assertiveness and aggression because she was always out to please everyone, seeking their approval to feel wanted; validated; loved. She was a people pleaser and also harbored a fear of abandonment. Susan also explained her inability to let go of Mike and her other ex who abused her was because of trauma bonding –

another new term Anna learned about herself. To Anna, this kind of wicked love was better than no love at all; it was better than being alone. Plus, the trauma bond kept her linked to Mike. This was a psychological response to abuse. It occured when the abused person formed an unhealthy bond with the person who abused them. This happens through a repeated cycle of abuse, devaluation, and positive reinforcement. And is very hard to break out of, which is why victims keep going back to their abusers, just like Anna – this was an eye-opening discovery she learned about herself.

Alone... unloved... worthless... unwanted... these feelings terrified her; if one man abandoned her, she had to find another to take his place... fill the void, save herself... from herself... love her, for she couldn't love herself. When you don't love and respect yourself you tend to fall into chaotic relationships. It was mentioned in the movie, *The Perks of Being a Wallflower: We accept the love we think we deserve* – this couldn't be more true.

It all made sense now, her suspectibilty to trauma bonds, her patterns, her infidelity, her need for love, intimacy, the alcohol abuse, her lack of self-respect, confidence, her impulsivity, the self-harm and her crazy twisted and confused mind and actions – everything.

There was a certain release to have finally found some answers. She hated herself for the things she had done to her body. Starving herself, year after year, to fit into a certain body type that was considered "beautiful". Hurting wonderful guys who didn't deserve the pain she inflicted on them. Hurting herself with the alcohol and the self-harm There was so much she hated about herself and the guilt would always seem to consume her because she could never let go of all the wrongs she had done.

Now that she had some clarity, she felt a weight lift off of her shoulders. Maybe now, she would be able to let go of her guilt, forgive herself and change her ways.

She didn't want to feel like a victim; no, she wasn't going to be the victim. She had a problem, and now she knew why. All she had to do was give it her all, to fix herself.

She was not about to point fingers and blame anyone for her mistakes. She loved her parents dearly and knew they did the best they could. Her dad wanted them to have a good life, so he worked hard to provide for them and it is because of him that she had such a comfortable life and she was thankful to him.

Her mum battled psychological disorders and she did the best she could. And it's not like she left Anna in a dumpster, she did care for Anna, cooked her healthy meals and took her shopping when she was younger, Anna knew her mum did love her, it was just these problems of the mind more than anything else, that took away her sweetness and left a bitter taste behind.

And all the 'no-s' that were ignored, all the strikes she had endured and all the hearts that she had broken along with hers, led her to this moment of realization and made her who she was right now in this moment. She was thankful for it all. It was not too late, and for once instead of running away she was going to stay.

With each session, she would heal her inner child, she would get a better sense of who she was and how she could make a wrong right. She felt very grateful to have found Susan.

The healing process had started. She had gone through four rounds of childhood regression therapy, but she knew there was a long way to go, and she was ready. She was not going to give up. She realized she just needed time for herself to figure out who she was without a man because she hadn't been single since high school. She honestly wanted to find out how she would manage without being in a relationship, without someone giving her constant love and affection; this nasty web of co- dependency is something she needed to break free from.

She wanted to be responsible for her own happiness and not depend on someone else to keep her stable and happy. Was she going to be able to do this? After fourteen years and a string of relationships, would she be able to be on her own? She'd just have to wait and find out. She needed to start her journey to self-discovery and self-love, it was her time now.

She still wanted to tell Adam everything once he was back. She hoped he would understand and give her time. She had asked for some space before but then had ended up going back to him because she was miserable alone, she hoped this time around things would be different.

She was on the way back from a late session on a Wednesday evening, feeling positive and uplifted. She had just finished talking to Adam as the car pulled up to her house. She stepped out and headed towards the lift. She was fiddling for her keys in her bag when she looked up to press the elevator button, that's when she saw him standing there, tall and strong with a sullen look on his face – Mike – Anna's heart rate doubled, her throat closed up her and her knees almost gave away.

"What are you doing here?" she managed to say. "We need to talk," came the curt reply. He held her hand and lead her towards the taxi waiting outside, she didn't protest because he had this way about him. When he was around, she felt powerless, in a good way… Was that even possible to feel in a good way?

He led her into the cab, but didn't say a word, she questioned him about their whereabouts a couple of times, but when he didn't reply, she knew it was better to let it go. They sat in silence for about thirty minutes until the cab pulled up at a hotel. He stepped out and she followed him to the reception, into the lift and into his room.

"Sit," he commanded. Anna sat in anticipation. "I'm sorry for everything I've ever done to you, for each time I've hurt you. I've loved you for eleven years now and that's all I know, you are my home; my oxygen and I don't know how to live without you," Mike paused, "I know I sometimes say and do things that are not to your liking, and they are wrong and I promise you they will never happen again, just give me one more chance and I'll never let you down again. I have some dents in my personality but who doesn't? I want you, Anna the whole of you, with the dents and the scars, because that's what makes you, you. And I wouldn't have it any other way… Can't you overlook my flaws too and accept me as I am? Individually we may not be the best, but we can fit together like the perfect pieces of a puzzle don't you think?" Mike questioned.

He then went on to begging and pleading with Anna to stay, telling her to give him one last and final chance. Mike was pleading and crying for her, and it hurt Anna to see him this way.

Anna was speechless, here he was the man of her dreams; her man, saying all the right words, everything she needed to hear. All she wanted to do was run into his arms and have him whisk her away to some corner of the earth, where it could just be the two of them, forever young.

However, she knew this was not possible practically; that reality would soon sweep over them like a storm and destroy everything in its path. He was saying all the right things now, but he was a narcissist trying to win her back to abuse her again, thus strengthening the trauma bond she was stuck in. This was the reality and she needed to accept it now and RUN in the other direction.

"I need time," she managed to croak.

And before Mike could stop her, she rushed out of his room, and out of the hotel, because she knew one look into his eyes; one touch and she would be his… all over again… after everything she had done so far, just so she could avoid that situation. She walked several blocks to clear her head until she finally decided to hail a cab. Her phone was constantly buzzing with Mike's calls, she picked it up and told him to have patience and that she would text once she got back home to let him know she's reached safely.

She thought about Adam… If she wasn't strong enough to break the bond and decided to go back to Mike, could she really give up a seven-year-long friendship for an eleven-year long love story?

Her heart belonged to Mike, but her soul belonged to Adam.

She reached home, took off her belly ring and was about to change into her pyjamas when her phone rang, it was Adam calling again, they had spoken on the phone earlier and said their goodnights, so why was he calling again? She hoped everything was alright. She picked up the phone with a touch of worry in her voice "Hey what's up? What happened?

Adam replied with a playful tone, "Look out of your window." Anna rushed to the window to find Adam and his motorbike parked right outside her house. Her first reaction was one of pure joy, the usual feeling she had every time she saw his face. But then, reality hit her and she had this horrible sensation in the pit of her stomach.

She snapped back to reality after re-living the incidents in her mind over the last two months.

She had to face this, she had to face him. "I'll be right down," she said. She changed back into her clothes and made her way downstairs. This felt like the longest walk of her life, it was as if time stood still, and all she could see were the memories collected over the years... with Adam, with Mike, with herself, flash in front of her eyes.

She had made it to the front door; she reached for the doorknob with sweaty palms, and turned the knob before she lost her nerve, and stepped out into the cold night.

There he was looking more handsome than ever in his dark blue jeans, white tee and suede jacket. The instant familiarity and comfort came rushing back to her, he was home for her, but Mike was the adventure, the thrill that kept her going back for more. But what was she to herself?

She had made a decision to tell Adam everything, but now she wondered if that was the best choice because she had a feeling, this time he wouldn't be there for her after all the heartbreak he had endured. What was she going to do? Tell Adam everything and lose him forever, choose him and never get to see Mike again, or just walk away from them both and learn to love herself? Her time had run out, she couldn't buy any more time from either of them or herself, she had to choose now. Either way, she was going to get hurt.

She walked up to him, he pulled her into his arms and hugged her so tight she just wanted to stay nestled in there forever. She stepped back looked into his eyes and said,

"We need to talk…"

1 Month Later

Chapter 21

ANNA

His face still haunted her, he looked completely distraught – he was shattered. He was crying while still holding the bag of gifts he had brought for her. She had broken his heart for the last time because this time all he said was, "enough," and walked away and didn't take her calls for weeks.

She had also told Mike that she couldn't do this any longer, and they both needed to let each other go, that had perhaps been the hardest phone call of her life. She had now cut off the two most valuable ties from her life; for the first time in fourteen years, she suddenly had no one to love her.

She felt lost and empty, she even came close to hurting herself again and going on an alcohol binge, but somehow, she restrained herself. It was always in the darkness and the silence of the night when she felt the loneliest. There were sleepless nights and nights when she cried herself to sleep. The only thing that helped her, were her sessions with Susan which now increased to four times a week. The time she spent with Sophie and Chrissy were also therapeutic.

But then there came a night, when she just couldn't take it anymore. It was 11 pm her parents were fast asleep, they hadn't a clue about what was going on with her because she would say she was going to work every day and instead go to Chrissy's house while she was supposed to be at work and stay there the whole day and then come back.

She tiptoed out of her room and headed for their bar, she took out a bottle of Scotch and went up to the roof. She looked up at the sky, she couldn't see any stars. The few lights from the neighbouring houses and streets were the only things sparkling in the darkness of the night.

She took a couple of sips, it burned her throat as it went down. The tears spilled and her heart raced… she suddenly felt there was nothing left anymore. She kept drinking until more than half the bottle was empty. In her heavily inebriated state she thought about Adam and Mike and all her past mistakes and pain – as the tears kept spilling out more and more.

With the bottle in hand she stood up and headed towards the edge of the roof, stumbling and falling all the way. She was dizzy, and the twinkling city lights now seemed hazy. She looked down and instantly lost her footing; she managed to keep her balance but dropped the bottle. She lost sight of the bottle and didn't hear it hit the ground; she wondered where it had fallen. Maybe it landed on the soft grass and didn't break after all, their roof wasn't too high.

She slowly got off the edge and decided to head down to find the bottle in case it hadn't broken, because she wanted to keep drinking. Her plan was to head back inside and pop some of her mother's sleeping pills that were lying in the medicine cabinet after that, and lie down on her bed, fall asleep and never wake up. This was how she was going to leave this world, cold and all alone with no one to love or hold.

She made it downstairs and quietly opened the door and headed towards the backyard. She knew the grass had grown quite a bit and the ground was moist due to the showers earlier that evening, so she had to tread carefully. It was quite dark and Anna had left her phone on the roof and couldn't use the torch light.

She decided to still give it a try to find the bottle as she desperately needed to drink more. She hadn't taken two steps, when she thought she saw something glistening in the grass in the dark; she paused… there it was again! Was she hallucinating? She saw it again; this was just like the treasure hunt of her childhood days. She decided to investigate further and took another step; she hit her foot on something tripped and fell on the grass.

What happened next was magical. As soon as Anna hit the grass, tiny specks of gold flew up from the grass and surrounded her. She blinked a couple of times and tried to see clearly. It took her a few seconds to realize that she was surrounded by hundreds of fireflies; they must have come out of hiding when she fell on the grass and disturbed them.

This year Chicago had seen an increase in the number of fireflies due to a wetter than usual spring, they loved damp surroundings and must have come into their backyard.

Anna watched these mystical lighting bugs while still lying on the grass. It was as if Mother Nature had put on her own show of fairy lights for Anna. She watched them with delight forgetting all about her quest to find the bottle of Scotch.

She suddenly thought of the song, *Fireflies by Owl City*, ten years ago she had told Jake that this song reminded her of him. They used to listen to it over and over again. This song encapsulated the times they shared together, all her memories with Jake came rushing back, it was if she had travelled back in time to 2009, how she wished she could do that just so see his face again. She hadn't heard the song in years, how did the lyrics go again? She tried to remember and through whispered voices started to sing… *Na na na …*

You would not believe your eyes if ten million fireflies lit up the world as I fell asleep… na na na…

Cause I'd get a thousand hugs from ten thousand lightning bugs as they tried to teach me how to dance… na na na…

I'd like to make myself believe that planet earth turns slowly it's hard to say that I'd rather stay awake when I'm asleep cause everything is never as it seems…

Things never were as they seemed… what was she doing? Maybe this was Jake; maybe it was the universe trying to tell her something… that her time wasn't up; this couldn't be the end; this was just the beginning. She knew then that she couldn't give up; she had to fight… fight hard this time… for herself.

So, she picked herself up off of the ground, stood up tall, smiled and danced with the fireflies.

1 Year Later

Chapter 22

ANNA

The sound of the alarm woke Anna up from her sleep. It was 8:30 am; she pulled the covers closer to herself and sunk in deeper underneath the warm blanket. The cold winter morning made it hard for Anna to get out of bed, but as she started drifting off again, she thought of him, and how he must be eagerly waiting for her.

The thought of keeping him waiting gave her the push she needed to get moving. She quickly got out and proceeded to get on with her morning chores. She was not a morning person, but meeting him always made her want to rush out the door no matter how early it was.

She got dressed and poured herself some cereal to-go, eating in the cab was not ideal, but it worked for her so she stuck with it. The Uber was almost here so she grabbed her lunch and headed out the door. She got in plugged in her headphones and had a spoonful of cereal.

After around forty minutes, she stepped out of the Uber and stood in front of the big black gate. The warm smile and morning wishes from the salt and pepper haired guard always made the day a little bit brighter. She greeted him as he unlocked the gate for her. She stepped onto the cobbled pathway that lead to the manor.

She took the first step towards the house and that's when she spotted him coming around from the back of the house; he had heard the gate open and knew she had arrived. He looked so handsome; she just wanted to run to him.

But before she could take another step, he was already running towards her. As soon he got close to her he jumped on her and started licking her face, with his tail wagging vigorously–Snuggles, the sweetest dog she had ever met. Meeting him every morning was what Anna looked forward to more than anything else every day.

After this (daily) morning ritual, Snuggles lead the way for Anna towards Mr and Mrs Baker who were standing by the house. "Good morning Anna! Ready to get to work, love?" asked Mr Baker in his usual chipper tone. "Yes, William," Anna said. "Come with me first love, there's something I need your help with," said Mrs Baker and took Anna out back.

The backyard was where all the love awaited her. Anna looked out at the big backyard which extended over five acres. The Bakers had managed to acquire the big chunk of land behind their house and turn it into a Doggie Day Care centre. This was Anna's office now. She mainly took care of all the content for the brand but also loved helping out with taking care of the dogs, from feeding to bathing to grooming them. She loved spending time with her furry friends.

This was a relatively small business but they had a loyal clientele. Mr and Mrs Baker had moved to Kolkata in their early 20s during the British Rule, in 1946. They fell in love with the city and never moved back and got their Indian citizenships to reside in India permanently. They lived in a beautiful colonial mansion which still stood strong today. Mr Baker worked as an accountant and Mrs Baker was a homemaker. They had two kids, Linda and Ben both of whom eventually married and moved away.

Both William and Alice Baker were kind people with a lot of love in their hearts for everyone; they made being human look easy, there was never any anger, or hatred; any greed or selfishness; just pure human emotions at its best.

After Mr Baker's retirement, a sense of sadness swept into their lives, the thought of not having anything more to do but wait for death, ate away at them every day. Sure, they would visit their children one living in the US and the other in Australia and their kids too would come down for the holidays with the grandkids, but eventually they would leave again...

And all their friends now in their early-seventies were great company but eventually those moments would also pass.

The idea of getting a dog was Mrs Baker's, they both loved animals especially dogs and decided they needed another member in the family to brighten up things around their home. That's when they got Snuggles a gorgeous, kind, loyal and loving Golden Retriever, who never left their side and brought with him all the joys in the world.

Their sadness and loneliness soon faded and eventually the idea of the Doggie Day Care was born. Anna was lucky to have become a part of their family.

She had moved to Kolkata one month after that eye-opening night in her backyard. She begged and pleaded with her parents to let her go back. She wanted a fresh start and she knew just where to find it – the beautiful yellow house of her childhood days. Luckily her parents hadn't sold it, and had instead kept a caretaker who used to come once a month for cleaning and maintenance.

After a lot of persuasion her parents agreed. Before leaving she met Chrissy, Sophie and Dan too. Dan and she, were in a better place now, he had just needed time and he had remained just a friend and never tried to ask her out again. And the last she heard from him a couple of days back was, he had a girlfriend now, and Anna was very happy for him.

Sophie and Chrissy were sad to see her go, but they knew, for Anna, this was the best. They promised to visit, and they did, just the previous month, what a reunion it was! She also met Adam; she wanted to thank him for everything he had ever done for her; she couldn't have asked for a better best friend. His love was innocent and pure. A kind of unconditional love that was hard to find now- a-days. She said she was sorry for everything and never meant to hurt him, he of course forgave her and even asked her to stay, but she told him how important it was for her to go.

So, he held her hand, and kissed her cheeks and said, *"Out beyond ideas of wrongdoing and right doing there is a field. I'll meet you there."* This was a famous quote by the poet Rumi, and Adam from time to time used to recite this to Anna in Hindi, and she loved hearing it; it was so beautiful especially the way he used to say it, it made her cry. Maybe someday they could be friends again. But for now, she was on her own.

She even flew down to meet Mike in Israel, as he had landed there after his flight and would be there for a couple of days. She said her thank you-s and sorry-s. He too wanted her to stay with him, and she really wanted to, but she knew she shouldn't. They hugged and kissed goodbye and when he finally let go, she saw tears in his eyes as he grazed his fingers along her sides to get one last feel of her.

Though her heart was broken, she did find some peace in knowing that she was finally able to choose herself… and she now knew, when her hair would grey and the wrinkles would frame her face, she would never forget this moment in her life.

After heading back to Chicago, she knew she had one last very important thing to do. She sat her parents down and spoke to them. Over the course of the year her relationship with her parents had improved. She opened up to them, and they listened – really listened. Maybe it was because they were older now in their late-sixties and had more patience and time and she was an adult and a lot saner than she had been in years! And as they say, distance makes the heart grow fonder— whatever the reason was, she knew now, she could always count on them, and that was the best feeling in the world.

On her last day in Chicago when she and her parents were at the airport, her mum cried while she was leaving. It justly made Anna feel her mother's love in the true sense after several years. It was something that she had always craved ever since she was old enough to understand the lack of it. She hugged her and cried too, but through the tears there was joy, joy in knowing her mum did love her somewhere deep down inside. She hugged her dad too with a lot of love and finally proceeded on her way, back to the place where she truly felt at home.

She took her seat on the flight and plugged in her headphones. The sweet symphony filled her ears …

"I'm coming home, I'm coming home, tell the world I'm coming home, let the rain wash away all the pain of yesterday, I know my

kingdom awaits and they forgiving my mistakes, I'm coming home, I'm coming home, tell the world I'm coming home..."

She smiled and looked out of the window; she was going to be just fine.